248

IN DANGER OF LOVE

Ellie and the Earl of Arlbury were virtual strangers, but in a war-torn country they were forced to rely on each other to survive. Outside the normal rules of their society they developed a strong bond which drew them ever closer. But then it looked as if their luck had finally run out, the dangers that had pursued them from the start seemed to have triumphed, and they were threatened by a final, tragic parting . . .

SHEILA HOLROYD

IN DANGER OF LOVE

Complete and Unabridged

LINFORD
Leicester

First published in Great Britain

First Linford Edition
published 2010

Copyright © 2009 by Sheila Holroyd
All rights reserved

British Library CIP Data

Holroyd, Sheila.
In danger of love. - -
(Linford romance library)
1. Love stories.
2. Large type books.
I. Title II. Series
823.9'2–dc22

ISBN 978–1–44480–109–5

1

Ellie was observing the Earl of Arlbury as he endeavoured to reassure the crowd of anxious questioners.

'You are in no danger,' he said firmly. 'The Duke of Monmouth is a foolish young man who is doomed to fail.'

'But he has landed with an army,' Lady Simbury said uncertainly.

'He landed at Lyme Regis with three hundred men — scarcely enough to conquer England,' was my lord's quick reply, but there were still doubters.

'Thousands have flocked to him since,' mumbled an unhappy-looking man.

'Artisans and farm workers armed with scythes,' Lord Arlbury said airily. 'They will soon fade away when the king's well-trained soldiers arrive to deal with them.'

In the face of such determined

optimism the interrogation faltered and conversation became more general, though it was clear that the worries still remained. Memories of the Civil War which had devastated so much of England were still too raw for people to treat lightly the Duke of Monmouth's recent arrival in the area with the declared intention of dethroning his uncle, King James, and claiming the crown of England as his own.

Ellie was prepared to admit — if anyone had thought her opinion worth having — that Lord Arlbury was carrying out his task very well. She would also concede that he was quite handsome, if not in the style she preferred. She could scarcely do otherwise, for it was not often that a noble adviser to His Majesty King James the Second deigned to travel from London's royal court to Somerset, and since his arrival two days before every woman in Simbury House had been in ecstasies over his appearance, dress, and general elegance.

Framed by his periwig, his face showed dark eyes, a nose that was straight, if a little long, and a well-shaped mouth above a firm chin. Ellie, however, thought his expression cold and patronising. Now, as Lord Arlbury conversed with the gentlefolk of the area, she stole a look at Harry Simbury from under lowered lashes and saw him smiling mischievously at her. She felt herself blush, and hurriedly transferred her attention back to Lord Arlbury, who was continuing in his endeavours to soothe the fears of those around him.

Tiring of all the talk about the rebellion, Ellie was wondering whether to slip away out into the garden to enjoy the summer evening when she realised that Harry was by her side.

'Shall we escape together?' he whispered, taking her by the elbow and steering her through the door, across the wide entrance hall and out into the flower-scented gardens. Once there he stretched his arms above his fair head and breathed in deeply, obviously glad to escape the anxious crowd.

'My Lord Arlbury talks well,' he said grudgingly, 'but anybody with any sense knows that he is here just to make sure the local gentry don't decide to support Monmouth.'

'Why should they?' Ellie enquired. 'The Duke of Monmouth is a bastard, even if he is a royal bastard. He has no valid claim to the throne.'

Harry shrugged. 'Monmouth is the eldest son of King Charles, and there are plenty of people who would prefer a Protestant bastard to a Catholic James.'

'Which would you choose?'

'My father will be faithful to King James because he regards him as the rightful king, regardless of his religion. I will also support James, because I don't think Monmouth can win. As Arlbury said, he brought three hundred men, but he brought very little in the way of arms to equip volunteers. So don't worry, Ellie. You are perfectly safe here.'

They strolled on through the gardens.

Ellie realised that one of his long arms was round her shoulders but made no attempt to dislodge it. Harry Simbury was her friend, her only friend at Simbury House, and she was very grateful to him.

When her mother had died leaving a five-year-old daughter, a neighbour had kindly offered to bring Ellie up with her own child while her father, Sir Walter Colinridge, had gratefully returned to the scholarly pursuits which his marriage had interrupted. The arrangement had worked well until the neighbour's daughter had married a year ago and it had been suggested to Sir Walter that it was time Ellie returned home and took charge of his household. Horrified at the idea of having his peace disturbed, he had persuaded Lord Simbury to take his daughter into the household in spite of Lady Simbury's reluctance. Her Ladyship was an efficient though cold guardian but her three blonde, extrovert daughters had soon been aware that their mother resented Ellie's presence and had amused themselves by finding various ways to make the quiet dark-haired girl with the hazel eyes unhappy. Harry, the heir and only son, had eventually realised that Ellie regarded him with shy admiration and this had led him to put an end to his sisters' more spiteful tricks and to favour Ellie with his company from time to time when nothing better offered.

Now she glanced up at him. 'If the rebels did advance — if they managed to take Bristol — would you be ready to fight them?'

His hesitation was momentary before he squared his narrow shoulders.

'Of course! Can you doubt it?' Then he relaxed. 'But it will not come to that. Lord Arlbury says that the king is sending four thousand soldiers — proper, trained men — to disperse the rabble. Your life will not be disturbed.' He changed the subject. 'I understand that Marian Foster is coming to stay for a few days tomorrow. She has just returned from London, so there will be plenty of gossip for you and my sisters.'

Lady Marian Foster was the spoilt heiress to an estate bordering the Simbury land, and while she might indeed be eager to discuss scandal and the latest fashions with Harry's sisters, she had so far ignored Ellie's existence to the best of her ability.

'It will be interesting to hear her news,' Ellie said as lightly as possible. 'Perhaps she has captured the heart of some courtier and is coming to tell us of her betrothal.'

Harry's confident step faltered and if Ellie had been looking, she would have seen that for a second his face betrayed a strange mixture of expressions. However he quickly summoned up a smile.

'Do you think the country mouse has captured some grandee?'

'I do not think she regards herself as a country mouse, and her inheritance should assure her of a good match.'

'Possibly,' Harry said casually. 'Now, let's forget about her. Tell me what you think of my fine new coat.'

He was obviously pleased by her praise of the garment, for when they turned to re-enter the house but were still hidden by the hedges, he bent to brush her cheek with his lips. Ellie's heart beat faster. It was the second time he had kissed her! He must be growing fond of her! Sometimes, very occasionally, she let herself dream of a future with Harry. After all, as the heiress to a respectable landowner, she would be a suitable match for him.

But for once this thought could not distract her for long. In spite of Harry and the earl's reassurances, she was still concerned about the possible danger threatened by the Duke of Monmouth. It might be 1685, but the Stuarts had only regained the throne of England twenty-five years earlier after the Civil War, the execution of Charles I, and the rule of Cromwell. Surely people would not allow the precarious peace and prosperity of the country to be threatened yet again!

But an eighteen-year old girl was not supposed to concern herself with matters of state, and the following day Ellie was doing her best to appear delighted to welcome Lady Marian Foster, who had appeared wearing a gown which Ellie privately thought far too ornate for a private gathering. Lady Marian was full of news, and full of herself. The young ladies of the household and Lady Simbury listened eagerly to her tales of court gatherings, handsome courtiers, and the extravagant purchases possible in London. Ellie thought privately that all the talk showed that Lady Marian had been admitted only to the most public of functions of the court, and that although she talked a great deal about what could be bought, she herself seemed to have returned with very little.

Ellie looked at Harry, who was sitting with his sisters and their guest, and wondered whether he was also noting the gap between reality and the impression Lady Marian wished to convey. However she was unable to catch his eye as he listened to the lady with apparent polite attention. She looked forward to hearing his comments later.

The door opened and attention was diverted momentarily from Lady Marian by the entrance of Lord Simbury and Lord Arlbury. Apparently Lord Simbury had decided that Lady Marian should be presented to the earl. Lady Marian was delighted and offered to bring the earl up-to-date with news of the court.

'I am most grateful for your offer,' Arlbury said politely, 'but in fact I left the court some days after your departure.' Ellie bent her head to conceal a smile as she remembered that the Earl had ridden to Somerset in great haste after King James II had been informed of Monmouth's arrival by two Lyme Regis customs officers, who had ridden the two hundred miles to London to warn him.

'I do not believe I have met this lady,' she heard Arlbury remark, and glanced up in surprise to find him looking at her. Lord Simbury beckoned her forward. 'May I present Mistress Elgiva Collinridge, Your Lordship. She is motherless, and my wife has been kind enough to let her join our household.'

Ellie curtsied, cheeks aflame.

'Elgiva? I have not met that name before.'

Ellie looked up, chin set defiantly.

'Elgiva was the name of an Anglo-Saxon queen, Your Lordship. My father is a scholar, devoted to the early history of England.'

'Indeed?' The polite rejoinder showed a complete lack of interest and the Earl turned his attention elsewhere, leaving Ellie wondering what to do and acutely conscious of the sniggers of the Simbury sisters and Lady Marian. Her attitude towards Lord Arlbury hardened into active dislike. If he was typical of the King's court, perhaps there was something to be said for supporting the Duke of Monmouth after all.

★ ★ ★

The following morning Ellie found that the rebellion seemed to have been forgotten as far as the Simbury family was concerned.

'Sir William and Lady Foster are calling today. Make sure you are wearing your best,' Lady Simbury instructed Ellie, who wondered what the fuss was about, as the Fosters were frequent visitors. There did seem to be an air of expectation, however, and one of the Simbury sisters condescended to inform her that it was a special occasion, though she refused to say why.

The Fosters arrived in the early afternoon and Sir William Foster was soon taken away by Lord Simbury for a private discussion. The two emerged after half-an-hour, both smiling broadly, and their family members were hastily summoned together. Ellie was included with the Simbury sisters. Sir William stood facing the small assembly, and after coughing to clear his throat and straightening his coat and cravat he commenced what was obviously a carefully prepared speech.

'All of you know the close friendship which has existed between our families for many years. Lord Simbury and I have worked together on many projects, and our wives are close and loving friends. I am therefore delighted to be able to announce that from now on our families will be linked even more closely.' He beckoned to his daughter and Lady Marian rose to stand beside him, simpering and giggling. 'After much careful discussion to ensure that our children will be happy and well-provided for, I have today given my consent to the marriage of my daughter Marian to Harry Simbury, the son of my old friend.'

Ellie felt as though someone had punched her. She could hardly breathe. She watched in a daze as Sir Walter summoned Harry to him and ceremonially linked the hands of the young couple. Then there was a roar of cheers and applause. Everybody surged forward to congratulate the pair. Automatically Ellie followed and wished them well, through stiff lips. Harry gave her a grin that was half-apologetic and half-triumphant.

As soon as she could, Ellie made her way to her own room and sank down miserably. Her tentative dreams of romance with Harry Simbury had been stupid and futile. The family negotiations would have been lengthy and intricate, so even when Harry was kissing her it had meant nothing to him because he must have known all the time that he was going to marry Marian Foster.

Ellie sent word by the maidservant that she was feeling unwell and would keep to her room that evening, and so she managed to avoid the celebrations and feasting that marked the betrothal. The next day she forced herself to rise and dress as normal. Life had to go on. She decided to go to the library and try to distract her thoughts with some of the leather-bound volumes which Lord

Simbury never touched, and was looking through a history of Wales when she heard the door open and lifted her head in surprise, it was Lady Marian Foster who entered, smiling.

'I was looking for you, Ellie, and Harry said I might find you here.' Her voice had never sounded so friendly. She advanced and laid a hand on Ellie's arm. 'I wanted to have a private word with you. Harry told me how he has behaved badly, trying to make you believe he cared for you — even kissing you, I believe — and he does feel a little guilty about it. But I told him not to worry. After all, you must have known you had no hope of attracting Harry.' The tone of friendship had gone now, replaced by spite. 'I have looks, money and good breeding. What could you offer?'

'Intelligence, perhaps?' Ellie retorted coldly.

Before Marian could reply, there was a polite cough and the two girls became aware that someone else had entered the library. Lord Arlbury was regarding the two of them with cold interest. Lady Marian hesitated, and then gave him a glittering smile. 'Lord Arlbury! I understand you were away yesterday so you won't have heard the news. Harry Simbury and I are betrothed. I was just telling Ellie that I am the most fortunate woman in the world and that I doubt if she can hope to find a match to equal him.'

Lord Arlbury's dark eyebrows rose.

'Harry Simbury? Oh, I remember — the spotty youth.' He turned to Ellie. 'I was told that you might be able to find me a decent map of the Bristol area.'

Marian Foster stood taken aback for a moment, realised that the earl no longer seemed aware of her existence, and made a hurried and rather undignified exit. Ellie quickly picked out a handful of maps and handed them to Arlbury.

'Thank you,' he said and spread them out on the desk. She did not move and he looked up, frowning. 'These will do.'

'You were unforgivably rude to Lady

Marian,' Ellie told him fiercely. He looked startled, then faintly amused.

'I am surprised that you are so ready to defend her. From what I heard, she was enjoying the fact that her future husband deliberately set out to mislead you and make you unhappy. I thought you would be pleased to see her triumph spoilt.' He turned back to the maps but Ellie did not move.

Finally he looked up again. 'What now?' he said wearily.

'You had no right to interfere. I don't need anyone else to fight my battles. How do you think it makes me feel, to know that a stranger is aware that I was a stupid fool who didn't realise I was being duped? I have been humiliated enough. All you have done is to give me an even worse opinion of you than I had before!'

He stared at her in amazement and then broke into unforced laughter.

'I hope that outburst has made you feel better. I apologise if you feel I behaved wrongly and, another time,

I will not come to your aid. Now, if you will please excuse me, I do have rather more important matters to deal with than the petty affairs of children.'

He returned to the maps with an air of finality. Ellie glared at him a moment longer before flouncing out of the door. As she made for the stairs to her room she heard a voice calling her name and Harry hurried towards her.

'Ellie, I must speak with you.'

'Go away, Harry! Go and have a good laugh with the lovely Lady Marian about my foolishness.'

'No! You must listen. What happened in the library? I've just met Marian and she won't speak to me. Honestly, I wasn't going to tell her about our friendship but she had noticed something — the way we looked at each other, perhaps — and then she dragged the details out of me. It wasn't my fault, Ellie — honestly.'

'You mean you took the chance to boast how you had amused yourself by trying to make me fall in love with you.

Well, let me tell you that I knew what you were doing and I was just playing you along. It was a game.'

Harry Simbury looked disconcerted, and then forced a smile.

'Then everything is all right!' He lowered his voice. 'Ellie, don't let this spoil our friendship. We had a special understanding, after all. Marian is a lovely girl, but there are aspects of me that she does not appreciate.'

Ellie looked at him with loathing.

'We were never friends. We were just amusing ourselves with each other. Perhaps Marian is lucky not to understand you as well as I do. At least she does not know that you are trying to get closer to another woman before the two of you are even married. Get out of my sight!'

This time she did escape to her own room where she threw herself on the bed and burst into tears. Afterwards she sat up and gloomily considered her future. Her dreams of romance were gone. Her father did not want her and soon she would be alone at the mercy of the Simbury sisters, their spitefulness doubtless encouraged by their new sister-in-law. Meanwhile, a few miles away, rebels were trying to bring a violent end to the country's legitimate government, as represented by the detestable Lord Arlbury. Her life could not possibly get worse, she told herself.

But it could, and the next day it did.

2

To Ellie's surprise, and greatly to her relief, the next day was quiet and uneventful. Lord Simbury and the Earl of Arlbury were riding through the country visiting the gentry, exhorting them to stay loyal to King James and assuring them that Monmouth's rebellion was doomed to early failure by giving them details of the royal army's progress. Their task was not easy. Seven thousand men had flocked to Monmouth's standard by now, and word had spread that they had defeated the local militia in some skirmishes.

Lady Marian had returned home with her parents and Harry had gone with them, invited to stay for a few days. Encouraged by their mother, his sisters were busy planning an ostentatious wedding for him whose many guests would include several possible suitors for themselves. Ellie had been left out of the discussions and busied herself with some sewing, vaguely aware of the life of the big house carrying on outside the morning room where the ladies of the house were assembled. Because of the Earl's presence, Simbury House had become the centre of the campaign against Monmouth and messengers were arriving all day, some with assurances of loyalty and some with worried requests for help. One of the main concerns of the local populace was the number of unscrupulous men who claimed to be followers of Monmouth but whose real intention was to seize the opportunities offered by the general unrest to raid and plunder vulnerable households.

The following day also started quietly enough. Lord Simbury and the Earl of Arlbury had returned after midnight and were spending the morning dealing with the news and messages that had arrived the previous day.

The storm broke shortly before

noon. A maid, almost running to deliver her message, told Ellie that her presence was required in the library as soon as possible — immediately, in fact. Puzzled, but aware of her clear conscience, Ellie made her way to the library where she found the two noblemen waiting for her. Her first thought was that they must require her knowledge of the library's contents to find some urgent information but it was immediately obvious that something else was the matter. Both men were standing by the desk which was littered with papers. The Earl, grimfaced and tight-lipped, acknowledged her arrival with a curt nod. Lord Simbury looked worried and flustered, with a letter grasped tightly in his hand.

'Elgiva, come in. We need to speak to you — perhaps you can explain . . . ' His voice tailed off, but his use of her full name showed that there was trouble. Suddenly he thrust the letter he held towards her. 'Can you explain this?'

Ellie recognised her father's scrawl. It was a very brief letter, in fact it consisted of a single sentence, but that was enough.

'I give my consent to the marriage of my only daughter, Elgiva, to Philip, Earl of Arlbury.'

Apart from the previous day's date and Sir Walter's signature, that was all. Ellie stared at it in disbelief, and then shook her head.

'What is this nonsense?'

'Exactly what I want to know,' Philip Arlbury said in cold, clipped tones. Looking at him, Ellie saw in his eyes the fury that he was trying to control.

'I know nothing about this letter,' she protested, but he cut her short.

'Are you sure? Or is this some stupid, childish device to embarrass me after the episode the other day?'

'You think I would do something like this?' She was instantly as furious as he was. 'Do you really think that I would lie to my father, tell him that I wanted to marry a man I had scarcely met, and do you think he would simply send his consent like this?' She turned to Lord Simbury. 'You know what my father is like. Tell him it is impossible.'

Lord Simbury spread his hands in despair.

'I would have thought so. But this is your father's handwriting and a messenger brought it from him yesterday. Lord Arlbury swears to me that he knows nothing about it.'

Ellie thought quickly.

'Then I would have had to have sent my father a request for his permission two days ago at the latest. I have not sent a message to my father for some time. Ask your servants.'

Lord Simbury looked even more bewildered.

'But in that case, why should your father write this?'

Ellie and Philip Arlbury looked at each other, both with the same thought. The earl turned to Lord Simbury.

'It does appear that the lady may after all be innocent in this matter. May

I ask you to confirm this by questioning your servants while I speak with her? Meanwhile, I shall be most grateful if you will not mention this to anyone.'

Thus politely dismissed from his own library, Lord Simbury left the two of them facing each other.

'Do you think Harry Simbury is responsible for this?' Arlbury asked directly. Ellie thought a while, frowning.

'He has played silly tricks in the past, for sure, but nothing like this, and I don't think he would risk the anger of his father and yourself. He has a strong sense of self-preservation.' She hesitated. 'And in truth I don't really think he is intelligent enough to devise such a plan.'

'Lady Marian Foster, then?'

'She would not have had the time to carry it out.'

'Then who is responsible?' He picked the letter up, frowning. 'Understand now, that I have not the slightest desire or intention of marrying you.'

'And I certainly do not wish to marry

you,' she said with sincerity.

'Continue to feel like that. I know I am regarded as a very desirable match, but there is no chance that I will feel that you have been so compromised that I will be obliged to ask you to marry me.'

'You may be the most eligible man in England but you are certainly the most conceited. You can be sure that you are quite safe from me,' Ellie said crisply.

They were staring at each other with mutual dislike when Lord Simbury hurried back into the room.

'Ellie is telling the truth. There has been no messenger from here to Sir Walter for the past three weeks.'

Philip Arlbury picked up Sir Walter's letter and thrust it into his pocket.

'Lord Simbury, Mistress Elgiva, please excuse me. I have His Majesty's affairs to see to. Then I shall investigate this matter further,' he announced, bowing formally.

When he had gone Lord Simbury sank into a chair, wiping his brow.

'Ellie, now it is just the two of us, can you assure me categorically that you know nothing about that letter?'

She nodded firmly and he sighed.

'Then why should your father write it? I know he is a little eccentric, but why should he do a thing like this?'

'My father is not mad, if that is what you are hinting,' Ellie said indignantly. 'You know that all he cares about is his study of the early history of England. I doubt if he had even heard of the Earl of Arlbury until something — or someone — made him write that letter.'

Lord Simbury groaned.

'I know that we are in for a very uncomfortable time. Arlbury will not rest until he finds out the truth.'

★　★　★

Ellie went to bed wondering what the next day would bring. In fact, it began to feel like a repetition of the previous day when she was once again summoned to the library, but this time she found only Philip Arlbury waiting for her and there was no sign of anger or indignation. Instead he greeted her politely with a bow and asked her to be seated. He stood before her with head bent and his hands locked behind his back until she began to wonder when he was going to speak, but finally he raised his head, cleared his throat, and began.

'I owe you an apology, Mistress Elgiva. I know now that you had nothing to do with your father's letter.'

'Then who did?' she demanded, without bothering to acknowledge the apology.

He sighed. 'This is where it becomes complicated. May I sit down?'

'Please do. Then tell me what you have found out.'

He pulled up a chair so that he was nearly facing her.

'First of all, what do you know about your Aunt Agatha?'

That was completely unexpected and she stared at him in bewilderment.

'My Aunt Agatha? I know virtually nothing. She was my mother's sister, but she disgraced the family by marrying a shopkeeper named Simpson whom she met on a visit to London, or so I have been told. She did call at my home once, I believe, when my mother was ill, but I was too young to remember her.'

'Anyway, she is dead now. My father received the news a week or so ago, together with the information that she had made me her heir, but my father doubted if she had anything to leave. I am not sure that he has even made any enquiries about the matter. How is she involved?'

The earl smiled wryly.

'In fact it appears that your information about your aunt is not quite correct. She married a merchant named Simpson, not a shopkeeper.'

'To my father, that would still have meant a tradesman, and he would not have wanted such a connection.'

'Master Simpson died some ten years

ago, and since then apparently your aunt has been living in London in very modest circumstances.'

Ellie started up, concerned.

'There was no need for that. Whatever my father thought of her social position, he would not have let a connection of his suffer. She should have written to him. He would have helped her!'

Arlbury held up a hand.

'There is no reason to feel sorry for her. According to her will, she could have lived in great comfort. From that it appears that her husband left her very well provided for. In short, Mistress Ellie, her will leaves you a fortune. You are now a very wealthy woman.'

She stared at him unbelievingly.

'But didn't anybody know that she was rich?'

'Apparently not. I don't know her motives for living in seeming poverty, but it makes no difference. She died rich and her money is now yours.' He sighed. 'Apparently the lawyer who dealt with her will decided that His Majesty, King James the Second, might be interested in the fact that there was now a wealthy and unmarried young heiress in his kingdom. He was.' Now Philip Arlbury held out a letter. 'His Majesty decided that I should be rewarded for my efforts to save his kingdom by the gift of a rich wife. He therefore wrote to your father asking him to consent to the match and to inform me of this consent. Your father obeyed the king and wrote the letter which you saw yesterday. James's letter to me was delayed and I received it this morning.'

Ellie shook her head to try to clear it.

'But no man, even if he is the king, can simply order two people to marry each other — surely.'

The earl's mouth twisted.

'James does believe that a king is all-powerful. Anyway, he must have believed that he was doing me a favour and that I would be delighted to be given a young, rich wife. He probably saw it as a reward for me which would have the added advantage of not costing him a penny personally. It does not seem to have occurred to him that I might not want to marry a colourless country mouse. I doubt whether he considered your feelings at all. In his opinion, women are supposed to do as their menfolk bid them, and should certainly obey a king.'

'But I do not want to marry you!'

'You made that quite clear yesterday,' Philip Arlbury commented. He lifted an eyebrow interrogatively. 'Are you quite sure you could not fancy me as a husband? I have been told that I am attractive to women, I have a distinguished title, and His Majesty is trusting me to help save his throne. Wouldn't you like to be the Countess of Arlbury instead of mere Mistress Ellie? Life at court is very expensive. Perhaps, on second thoughts, I could do with a wealthy wife.'

Ellie stared at him with horror.

'You can have the money without

marrying me! I'll give it to you! After all, I didn't know I was rich so I won't miss it!'

To her surprise, he burst into laughter and she stared at him indignantly till he regained his composure.

'Mistress Ellie, you may rest easy and keep your money. I don't need it, I have enough of my own and when I marry I will choose my own wife.' He smiled broadly. 'However, I must say that your obvious horror at the idea of marriage to me is damaging my self-esteem considerably. I can assure you that there are dozens of women who would leap at the chance to marry me.'

Ellie tried to pull her wits together.

'I am sure there are, and that they would think me mad not to want you as my husband, but as you must realise we are not suited. We would not be happy together. And incidentally I am not at all well pleased to have been called a 'colourless country mouse'!'

He nodded, once again serious.

'I apologise again. The question is,

what do we do about the situation? Your father seems to have given his consent very rapidly without even showing any desire to meet me. Could you persuade him to withdraw his consent?'

Ellie imagined herself confronting her father and closed her eyes in horror.

'I think my father gave his consent because he would feel duty bound to do whatever his king wished, and he would expect me to do the same.' Her voice grew bitter. 'He would also be delighted to think that someone else, my husband, would assume responsibility for me because he could then forget about my existence with an easy conscience. If I told him I did not want to marry you, he would be very angry.'

'Sometime you must tell me more about this strange father of yours. Meanwhile, if he will not help us, then somehow I will have to convince the king that our marriage would be a mistake — but personal concerns will have to wait till we have dealt with the threat of Monmouth. I will tell Lord

Simbury once again to keep the matter secret.'

'Even from Lady Simbury?'

'Particularly from Lady Simbury.' Philip Arlbury looked at Ellie thoughtfully. 'Whatever happens to the two of us, I think you must realise that your life is going to be very different in future now you are such a wealthy young woman.'

Her eyes widened.

'Do you mean that I am really rich? I can just go out and buy myself new gowns whenever I like?'

'You can buy gowns, jewellery, houses — whatever you desire. As soon as news of your inheritance gets out, you will have fortune-hunters from all over the country hurrying here to try to win your hand.'

She bit her lip.

'Do you think that if that information had been common knowledge a few days ago, Harry Simbury might have acted differently?'

'Are you asking me whether Harry

Simbury would have asked you to marry him and not Lady Marian Foster if he had known of your inheritance? It is very possible. Do you regret that he didn't?'

'No! I have had a lucky escape. I have realised that I only thought I cared for him because he was the first — the only — young man to show any interest in me. When he does learn that I am rich, I hope only that he will bitterly regret the way he has treated me.'

'So do I. He is an unpleasant youth and he and Lady Marian deserve each other. Now, forget him. It might help matters if we could avoid meeting as much as possible. I am obliged to keep Simbury House as the centre of my operations, unfortunately. Is there anywhere you could go, apart from your father's house?'

Ellie's face lit up.

'I could visit Mary Danbury. We were brought up together as sisters for many years until she married. She is expecting her first child and has asked me more than once to go to stay with her, and in fact I was planning to go this week but Lady Simbury thought Monmouth's rebels would make the journey dangerous. The Danburys live on the River Parrett. What do you think?'

Arlbury pondered the question for a while.

'My informants say that Monmouth is further south. I can send you with an armed escort and you should be safe enough once you are there. Monmouth does not want to antagonise the gentry by attacking their houses.'

Ellie clapped her hands in delight.

'Thank you so much! I will tell Lady Simbury immediately and it will not take me much time to pack.'

Philip Arlbury smiled wryly.

'I am glad I can make you so happy. Well, this may be the last time we see each other, Mistress Ellie. Even if we do not want to marry each other, I hope we can part on good terms. I may not want you as my bride, but you are certainly not colourless, nor mouse-like.'

Ellie smiled at him warmly.

'Thank you. And I will even say that when you do marry, the lady you choose will be very fortunate — if she marries you of her own free will.'

3

Ellie rode away from Simbury House the next day with a pleasant sense of adventure. She was, after all, going nearer the rebel forces, although the half-dozen troopers who escorted her assured her safety and all information indicated that the Danburys' home would be untouched by the disturbances.

'We'll have no trouble on the journey,' the sergeant assured her, and then grinned. 'Coming back may be more exciting for us. We are under instructions to try to find out exactly what the rebels are up to and where they are aiming for. We'll see how those country lads can fight against trained soldiers.'

So she had no reason, she realised, to feel guilty about diverting the soldiers from more important missions. Arlbury had decided they could simply combine two tasks. He was efficient. She could safely leave him to sort out their personal entanglement.

The group reached Danbury Manor after a few uneventful hours and as the horses clattered up the drive the front door opened and Mary hurried out to greet her friend.

Ellie and the former Mary Pontin had been born within a month of each other. Mary had also been an only child and when Ellie's mother had died it had been Lady Pontin who had welcomed Ellie into her household. She had treated her as Mary's sister for twelve happy years until Daniel Danbury had come courting, married Mary and taken her away to his house by the River Parrett. After the coldness and indifference shown her by the Simbury sisters, Ellie welcomed the warmth and kindness of her old friend's greeting. As her grooms led the soldiers and their horses round to the stables, Mary was urging her friend into the house.

'I'm so glad you could come! We haven't had any visitors since these troubles started and I've been longing to show you what we have done with the nursery.' She stopped and patted her stomach. 'Only a few months now! I'm sure it is a boy because he's started kicking already.'

Inside, her husband Daniel had been waiting in the drawing room for their guest to appear and greeted her with a warm smile in his grey eyes. His features were pleasant, if not handsome, and he and Mary were a happy, devoted couple.

'Welcome, Mistress Ellie! Sit down and let the servant bring you a glass of wine. Mary, I won't let you drag the poor girl off to see the nursery until she has rested after her journey.'

His wife pouted with assumed displeasure.

'Daniel, don't you understand that Ellie has come all this way specially to see the arrangements I have made for our child?'

Daniel embraced Mary fondly.

'I know, my dear, but first of all I want to talk to her. Ellie — as Mary said, we have been cooped up here since Monmouth landed at Lyme Regis a fortnight ago, and all we have heard are rumours. Now, I understand King James has sent the Earl of Arlbury to organise the opposition to the rebels. Can you tell us what is happening?'

'The earl is staying at Simbury House and he does seem very capable, but I don't know many details of the present situation. I understand the rebels are moving towards Bristol, hoping to take the city and open the port to reinforcements from Europe. If they fail, then they will find it difficult to face the king's soldiers when they arrive.'

Daniel thanked her for the news, but although he did not ask any more questions she could see that he was disturbed. Even if the rebels were defeated, they could still cause havoc as they retreated through the countryside and Daniel had his pregnant wife to worry about.

After the refreshments had been consumed, Ellie duly admired the refurbished nursery and all Mary's other preparations, but the time came when even Mary could think of nothing more to say about the approaching birth and turned to other subjects.

'What is the Earl of Arlbury like?' she asked with interest. 'Does he behave like a great lord?'

Ellie shrugged.

'He has great confidence in himself, but I am not sure whether that comes from his birth or his awareness of his own talents.'

'It sounds as though you don't like him,' Mary commented.

'True. I think he is intelligent and capable, but I do not like him. In fact, after the few dealings we have had with each other I would say the dislike is mutual.'

'What dealings? What has happened between you?'

Ellie hesitated, longing to tell her dear friend about the king's arbitrary decision that she should marry the earl and Arlbury's reaction, but she managed to restrain herself. The fewer people who knew about that problem the better. Instead she diverted Mary by informing her that there was a possibility that her Aunt Agatha might have left her a tidy sum of money. Mary sat up.

'You mean you may be rich?'

'Let us say comfortably off. Anyway, my father will be in charge of my affairs and my money for some time yet.'

'Until you marry,' Mary pointed out, and her expression grew pensive. 'You will be a very good match now, Ellie. I must think of a suitable husband for you.' A thought struck her. 'You have met Daniel's brother Jonathan, haven't you?'

'Don't try to marry me off before I'm even sure my aunt has left me anything!' Ellie retorted, but Mary's reaction to the news reminded her of

Arlbury's warning that her life would never be the same again.

The following two days were a pleasant interlude. Ellie and Mary embroidered gowns and little caps for the baby and gossiped happily. Daniel took the opportunity, when Mary was busy discussing menus with the cook, to have a word with Ellie.

'Lady Pontin plans to be here for the birth and will stay for at least a week afterwards, but she has her own household to run. If it doesn't interfere with your plans too much, I should be most grateful if you would stay here when she has to leave. You are a very competent young woman.'

Ellie smiled gratefully.

'I would love to stay, and I am sure Lady Simbury won't miss me.'

'No, I gather from Mary that you are not entirely happy there. Perhaps I should have invited you to make your home with us when Mary and I married.'

'What an idea, Daniel! As newly-weds you didn't want a third person with you all the time!'

'I admit that is true.' His smile transformed his face. 'But now we are an old married couple, and soon to be parents, you are certainly welcome here for as long as you like.'

'I shall remember that,' Ellie said gratefully. It would solve the problem of staying away from Simbury House and any contact with the Earl of Arlbury.

★   ★   ★

In spite of the apparent peacefulness of the area, Daniel made sure his menservants went about armed and at least four of them were always guarding the approaches to the house, ready to give warning if strangers were seen. On the third day there was a sudden commotion outside the house and Ellie and Mary reached the door just as one of the guards began to hammer on it. He was supporting a white-faced man who seemed on the point of collapse. At the sight of him, Mary gasped and sat down heavily on a chair. She seemed about to faint. Ellie looked round, saw Mary's maid staring open-mouthed at the spectacle and ordered her to look after her mistress. Then she directed the guard to take the man into the morning-room and sit him in an armchair, and then instruct the butler to bring some brandy. The man was obviously near to exhaustion, but grasped at her gown.

'Master Danbury — I must speak to him.'

Before she could reply, Daniel himself came in, hurriedly summoned from the stables. The man struggled to sit up when he saw him.

'Master Danbury, I was trying to find you! The rebels — they attacked the farm this morning — I managed to get out without their seeing me and came here as fast as I could.'

Daniel bent over him. 'Sit back and rest. You did the sensible thing, to come here for help. Now, you're Jonty from the Mathers' farm, aren't you? How many attacked you?'

'Half-a-dozen men on foot armed with muskets and pistols. Farmer Mather and his wife and their young lad were the only people there besides me. Please will you help them?'

Daniel's lips tightened. 'Half-a-dozen? It sounds like a gang of marauders, not soldiers. My men and I can deal with those.' He turned to Ellie. 'We have been lucky so far but it looks as if the war has finally reached us. I must go. Can you look after this poor man? I'll leave a couple of guards here with you.' He looked round. 'Where is Mary?' he said with sudden, sharp anxiety.

'She is well, but she was shocked. I can cope. You go and help those poor people,' Ellie told him, trying to sound confident and relieved to see the butler finally arriving with the brandy.

Daniel still hesitated.

'These people are my neighbours and friends. They would help me if I were in danger. I expect the attackers won't be prepared to face my men.'

'I am sure you are right, and the sooner you go, the sooner you can help them.' Ellie spoke with calm determination.

Daniel strode out, shouting instructions to his servants as she poured some of the spirit into a glass and held it to the messenger's lips.

Later Ellie found Mary huddled in a chair in the drawing-room. She gave a woeful little smile when her friend came in but her face was tear-stained.

'I'm sorry, Ellie. It was stupid of me to feel so faint, but I was frightened. How is the poor man?'

'He is suffering from exhaustion more than anything. We gave him a sleeping draught and put him to bed.' She looked down at Mary affectionately. 'You can't panic over every little thing. What are you going to do when your child falls over and scrapes his knee?'

'Scream and send for you!' Mary managed to return, and then her face twisted and she looked about to burst into tears again. 'And Daniel has gone riding off to face a gang of desperate men! Suppose he is wounded or . . . ?'

Instead of finishing the sentence she sobbed loudly. Ellie sighed.

'Stop distressing yourself, Mary. It is bad for the baby. Daniel has ridden off surrounded by a dozen armed men to deal with some robbers who will probably run away at the mere sight of a horseman.'

Patiently she set herself to reassure Mary and persuade her that Daniel would soon return as a hero. That done, she moved on to what Mary should do to welcome him back after his successful foray.

'I'll have a special dinner prepared for him,' Mary decided. 'I'll instruct the cook to prepare his favourite dishes.'

The cook was summoned and she and her mistress spent some time deciding what should and could be prepared. Mary announced that she herself would gather the necessary herbs.

'You haven't seen my beautiful herb garden yet, have you, Ellie? Of course, it is not properly mature yet, but still I am very proud of it.'

'Are you quite sure you feel well enough to show me? It can wait until later.'

'Of course I do,' Mary protested, though her friend noticed she was still supporting herself with one hand on the arm of her chair. 'I'm sorry I was so silly. It was just so unexpected.'

Slowly, with Mary obviously grateful to be able to lean on Ellie's arm, the two young women made their way to the quiet corner of the garden where Mary had been lovingly cultivating herbs. Carefully they selected those which would be needed in the kitchen, but instead of taking them straight back to the house they settled on a sunlit bench in the shelter of a hedge.

'I have been so happy this year with Daniel in our own home, and so glad we are going to have a child,' Mary said apologetically. 'Then we heard the awful news that rebels had landed not far from here, and it seemed to me suddenly that my happiness was very fragile and could easily be destroyed. My grandfather was killed in the Civil War by Cromwell's troops and his house was burnt down. Since Monmouth landed I have been terribly afraid that the same thing would happen to me and Daniel, and when that man appeared this morning I felt that he was bringing ill-fortune to us.'

Ellie put her arm round her.

'Of course you are anxious, especially in your condition, but these rebels are a ramshackle lot, not like Cromwell's troopers. Don't worry any more.'

Mary leant against her gratefully.

'You're so sensible. If my baby is a girl I will name her after you.'

'You will not! I know how cruel it is to call a child Elgiva!'

Mary laughed shakily. 'Perhaps I will think again.' She picked up the basket where they had put the bunches of herbs. 'We'd better get these to the kitchen.'

As they turned towards the gate that led out of the walled kitchen garden they suddenly heard noises coming from the direction of the house. Mary halted, her eyes wide with fear.

'That will be Daniel returning,' Ellie said hastily. 'Let us go and see what has happened. He may have brought the Mathers family for us to look after. They have had a terrible experience.'

Thus reminded of her duties as mistress of the house, Mary started to hurry, but then both girls were stopped in their tracks by a new sound. Musket shots were being fired. Then the crack of pistols could be heard. Mary turned a white, frightened face towards her friend. They had reached the main path that led up to the house and as they stared towards it one of the footmen appeared, running towards them. He was shouting, possibly a warning to his mistress, but while he was still some distance away there was a single musket shot and he fell to the ground. Mary gave a piercing scream, dropped the basket of herbs, and turned and ran as fast as her long skirts would allow.

'Mary! Stop!'

Ellie gathered up her skirts and ran after her friend. Then she heard more shots behind her, and suddenly running away seemed a good idea. The two girls reached the garden limits and scrambled through the small gate which was used by the gardeners.

'We must get down to the river. We can hide there,' Mary shouted back without slowing her headlong rush.

Ellie caught her up and tried to restrain her, but Mary tore herself free and ran blindly on through the scrub and woods that bordered the River Parrett, until finally she slid down the slope that led to the river and sank into a huddled heap by the water's edge. Ellie, panting and breathless, scrambled down beside her.

'We must hide,' Mary insisted fearfully. 'Perhaps we can find a cave.'

Ellie didn't find a cave, but there was a hollow behind a curtain of ferns where the overhanging bank provided some shelter. Here Mary collapsed on the floor while Ellie inspected their refuge. The hollow was small and dry and secret. For the time being they were safe, and for a while they rested in silence, but Ellie realised that this could only be a temporary hiding place.

'Do you think the people attacking our house were the same group who attacked the Mathers?' Mary said finally.

Ellie thought for a while. If it was the same group, then its members must have met and defeated Daniel and his men — and she did not want Mary to think about that possibility. Finally she shook her head.

'That man from the farm said about six men attacked the Mathers. That wouldn't have been enough to attack your house.' She tried to sound cheerful and positive. 'Well, whoever they are, they are in for a nasty shock when Daniel gets back with his men. He'll have them running in minutes.'

'How will we know?' Mary interrupted. 'If we go back, we might find the rebels are still there. They might capture us!'

'We'll wait till it is dark,' Ellie told her. 'Then you can stay here while I creep back and see what the situation is. I'll probably be back within the hour, with Daniel, to take you home.'

Mary shivered and looked around her.

'Meanwhile this cave may be safe, but it's cold and dark, and we haven't anything to eat,' she said plaintively.

Ellie hugged her, secretly wishing that her friend had a little more spirit.

'Don't be silly. Daniel will come back, clear the house, and then come looking for us. All we have to do is wait for him.'

They waited, huddled together for warmth. Gradually, as the hours passed, they began to nod. Ellie woke suddenly and started to her feet. The declining sun showed that it was late afternoon. Mary sat up. Somewhere, outside, there were noises. Listening carefully, they could distinguish the sound of oars and a man's voice, shouting. Gradually it became clearer.

'Mary! Where are you? Mary!'

It was Daniel Danbury, come to seek his wife. In seconds the girls were standing on the river bank, waving to attract attention.

'Daniel! Daniel! We are here!' Mary cried shrilly.

On the river they could see a small boat with three occupants. One man was rowing, another was sitting scanning the banks, and Daniel was standing upright.

'Daniel!' Mary cried again, and they saw his face turn towards them. He pointed to where they were standing. Mary held out her arms to her husband, tears of joy running down her face. Rapidly the oarsman drove the boat towards them. But then, when the boat was only a few yards away, there was a sudden volley of musket shots from somewhere nearby, the musket balls splashing into the water near the boat. As the boat grounded on the river bank, the seated figure stood up and leapt out into the thigh-deep water. Ellie pushed Mary towards the boat where her husband was waiting. There was another ragged volley and the man standing in the water cursed, grasped Mary, lifted her, and bundled her into Daniel's arms.

'Take your wife and go before they get any nearer!' the man ordered and backed up his words by thrusting against the boat with all his might, launching it back into the river. The oarsman bent to his work, eager to get the boat out of range. The man turned back to Ellie, who took a deep breath and was about to speak when she was seized and thrust to the ground, where the weight of the man's body held her down.

'Keep absolutely quiet or you'll get us both killed,' hissed a voice in her ear.

It was Philip, Earl of Arlbury.

4

Ellie was finding it difficult to breathe and fought to lift her head, only to have a hand clamped over her mouth.

'Don't move, and keep quiet! It is our only hope.'

The urgency of his voice was convincing and she lay still obediently. For some time nothing happened, and then she heard bushes rustling and voices raised in argument.

'There's nothing here. I told you,' said one voice.

'Then why did the boat try to land here?' came an exasperated enquiry.

'One of them probably intended to come ashore for some reason. Obviously they were searching for someone, but whoever it was, I don't think they are round here.'

There was an interval and then the second speaker said reluctantly, 'I suppose you are right. Anyway, I can't see anything and I'm tired of stumbling through these thorn-ridden bushes.'

The noise and the voices grew fainter but it was some minutes before Philip Arlbury cautiously released Ellie, warning her again to make as little noise as possible, and they both sat up.

'Why on earth did you push the boat away?' she said in a furious whisper. 'We could have escaped. Now we are stranded here.'

He grunted impatiently.

'Those marauders were behind that rise over there. They could see the boat on the water but they could not see the stretch where we landed and the light was too poor for them to realise that one person had replaced another. As far as they are concerned, they saw three people arrive in a boat and three people leave in it. If you want to know why I didn't throw you into the boat after Mistress Danbury, it was because one more passenger would have weighed the boat down and slowed it so dangerously that it would have been a virtual sitting target for those muskets.'

'I didn't think of that,' Ellie said slowly.

He gave her a look of dislike.

'Do you think I should have saved you, rather than Mistress Danbury?'

'No, of course not! If you had to make a choice, then it was imperative to save Daniel's wife and child.' She looked around at the gathering darkness. 'What do we do now?'

'Wait until it is properly dark and then try and make our way back — and hope that those men are not between us and Danbury.'

Ellie was shivering with cold, as well as in reaction to the recent danger. She felt a cloak being wrapped around her shoulders and murmured her thanks.

'How did you come to be with Daniel Danbury anyway?' she asked.

'I had received word that gangs of robbers were attacking isolated farms and houses and I set out from Simbury House with some of my men to hunt them down. We found Master Daniel at a farm — Mather's farm, I believe. It had been attacked and looted earlier in the day, though the family was not harmed, and the attackers had gone. Danbury invited us to stay at his house for the night and when we got there, we found that his servants had just managed to see off another gang of rascals. Only one of his men was hurt but everything was in chaos. Danbury and his servants had scoured the house and gardens for you and his wife, but you could not be found.'

'Then someone discovered an abandoned basket of herbs near the edge of the gardens and we decided you must have fled through the woods towards the river. Danbury and I decided to take the boat on the river as it seemed a way of finding you as quickly as possible. You know, there was really no need for you to run away,' he finished irritably.

'We saw a man fall after he had been shot, and then Mary panicked and ran

on and on and I had to go with her,'
Ellie explained. 'I am glad that the
house is safe. Mary loves it, and has her
heart set on giving birth there.'

Philip Arlbury gave a half-laugh.

'Well, let us hope there are no more
attacks on it. Meanwhile there are even
more important matters to be taken
care of urgently as far as we are
concerned. We'll wait another hour.'

They sat in silence until he murmured, 'It is dark enough. I think we
can move safely now. Follow me
closely.'

It was difficult to obey him. In the
woods it was almost too dark to see
their way, and while Philip's boots
crushed the plants beneath his feet,
Ellie kept tripping over roots. Soon she
was exhausted and finding it difficult to
keep up with him. At last, just as she
was beginning to think she would have
to beg him for a rest, Philip halted. He
was staring in the direction of Danbury
Manor. Following his gaze, Ellie was
dismayed to see a red glow in the sky

and it was just possible to hear the rattle of musketry.

'Unfortunately it looks as though Danbury has been attacked again, and this time by a much larger force!'

Ellie stared at the glow, appalled as she thought of what might be happening to Mary and Daniel.

'It's on fire! Mary and Daniel — they may have been killed!'

Her voice rose shrilly and his fingers bit into her shoulders as he seized her.

'Quiet! Don't be so foolish. Danbury has men to defend it. A few flames mean nothing. Perhaps Daniel decided to move to the safety of a town and the raiders are burning an empty house.'

'But what can we do now?'

She saw his silhouetted shoulders shrug.

'Well, we can't go to Danbury Manor when we don't know who would be there to greet us. If I were by myself I could try to get nearer to see what is happening there, but it would be difficult, and hopeless with you in tow.'

At that moment they heard the heavy tramp of booted men and Philip grasped Ellie's arm and pulled her into the woods. As they crouched behind some bushes a small party of men made their way along the track they had been following, going towards the river. There was just enough moonlight to see the muskets on their shoulders. Philip Arlbury was cursing steadily under his breath.

'They may be the men who attacked the Mathers. We dare not risk travelling further now in case there are other armed groups around and we stumble across them. We'll have to try and find somewhere to spend the night.'

A few minutes later they came across a low, half-ruined building which had been intended to shelter animals, not humans.

'I'm afraid this is the best we can do for the night,' Arlbury commented.

At least it was dry, and the rough stone walls gave shelter from the wind. Ellie sank down while Philip stood fumbling in his pockets — first for flint and steel, which he used to ignite a few sticks which gave a little light but no warmth. Then he passed her a flask.

'Have a mouthful of this.'

It was brandy and she swallowed the strong spirit, grateful for the warmth it spread through her body. When she handed the flask back she received in exchange a lump of bread, some cheese and a withered apple.

'You came well prepared!' she commented.

'I fought in the Low Countries for some years, and learned there that food is as important as ammunition for a soldier.'

'So you have been a soldier as well as a courtier?'

'I have attended the courts of King Charles and his brother, King James, but I would not call myself a courtier. Petty intrigues do not interest me and I do not need favours from the king.'

'But you are here at his request.'

'I am here for the sake of the

country, not the king. England could not stand the ravages of another Civil War.'

Crouched on the ground, now that they seemed to be safe for a little while, her thoughts went back to Danbury.

'Do you really think that Mary and Daniel have survived?' she asked fearfully. Arlbury's face was bleak.

'If they have been harmed, I swear to you that I will avenge them.'

In spite of the situation in which she found herself, and her fears for her friends, Ellie could not repress a yawn and her companion chuckled.

'Time for bed. Tomorrow will not be easy, so we need all the rest we can get.'

Dead weeds and some ancient hay had accumulated by one wall and Ellie lay down on it, clutching the cloak round her for a little warmth. Philip Arlbury extinguished the little fire and stretched out on the bare, stony earth. She heard him shifting uneasily in a vain attempt to get comfortable.

'My lord,' she said after some

minutes, 'I think it would be better for both of us if you came across here. Your proximity will keep me warm, and you will rest more easily on this hay.'

He sat up and then hesitated.

'Are you quite sure?'

'Yes,' she said with some asperity. 'I have more sense than to think you would try to ravish me.'

'After today's events, I don't have the energy, let alone the desire,' he commented wryly, coming to lie down by her side.

Ellie woke a couple of times in the night and heard him snoring gently by her side. It was strangely comforting.

★ ★ ★

When Ellie awoke, Arlbury was gone and she sat up in a panic. She relaxed as he re-entered the hut.

'There is a stream just over there,' he indicated. 'It is cold, but refreshing.'

Obediently she went out and splashed water on her face, drying it with her skirt. When she got back he had carefully divided the remaining bread and apples. It was enough to stop their empty stomachs complaining, even if the bread was stale. Philip Arlbury turned to her when they had finished.

'Now we have to decide where to go.'

'Back to Danbury?'

He shook his head regretfully.

'Danbury may not have survived, and we know not how many groups of rebels are roaming the area. Today there may be many more. We heard yesterday that Monmouth had reached Bristol too late, and that Lord Feversham was already there with men of the king's army, so the rebels cannot receive reinforcements before the bulk of the king's forces arrive. Many of Monmouth's recruits are deserting him, and there will be armed fugitives everywhere. Monmouth's men are facing defeat and death and such desperate men will show no mercy to travellers going east to reach the king's forces.'

'Surely they won't dare to attack the

great Earl of Arlbury?'

'That is a very silly remark.' He gave her a contemptuous look.

'I know! I'm sorry. But I am frightened!'

'Well, you have some cause to be.' His voice softened slightly. 'You have done very well so far. I expected you to spend the whole of last night in tears.'

'I could still weep, if you like,' she said with a shaky smile.

'I would be obliged if you refrained.'

'So where can we go?'

'We can go where the fugitives are going — back towards Taunton and Lyme Regis.' He held up a hand to forestall her protests. 'Believe me, it is the safest way. If we go towards Danbury or Bristol it will be obvious to anyone we meet that we are on the side of the king. If we go towards Taunton or Bridgewater we will become just two more people trying to escape Feversham. In addition, I know the names of people faithful to the king who stayed in those towns and who will help us if we can reach them.'

Ellie gulped. 'How long will it take us to get there?'

'A day — it depends.'

'But if we meet any rebels, they will see that we are not the kind of people to be fleeing on foot. Why should two members of the gentry be running away?'

He raised an eyebrow.

'Look at me. Do I look like a gentleman?'

She fell silent as she inspected him. He had not worn his wig for this rescue expedition and his close-cropped black hair resembled that of hundreds of ordinary citizens. He was unshaven and his dark practical clothes showed the effects of tramping through woodland and then sleeping on a pile of dusty hay.

She shook her head and then looked down at her own crumpled and dirty clothes before patting her uncombed hair. He grinned.

'I look like an adventurer who followed Monmouth from France and knows that his gamble has failed. You, my dear Elgiva, certainly do not look like a respectable gentlewoman.'

She looked at him bitterly.

'So I have no alternative but to tramp after you like a common soldier's woman and hope for the best.'

Philip's laughter was genuine and unforced.

'Hope for the best and do everything I tell you. Then we may survive. Incidentally, from now on we had better be Philip and Ellie to each other.'

★ ★ ★

It was a cloudy, dismal day with occasional showers of spiteful raindrops. Ellie huddled in Philip Arlbury's cloak and gritted her teeth as her feet grew more and more tired and painful. They followed minor paths as much as possible. Twice they stopped, hearing voices, but saw no one. The vegetation grew sparser and Philip was frowning as he looked around.

73

'We can't hide in this wasteland, but at least we shall be able to see other travellers before we meet them. In that case, allow me do the talking.'

In due course their path joined a slightly wider track which then led them on towards a junction with a rough road. At the crossroads stood a primitive alehouse, sheltered by a few windblown trees. A rough cart stood outside.

'We may be able to get help here,' Philip said shortly. 'I'll go in first to see whether it is safe.'

He strode towards the building, bending his tall head to pass through the low doorway. After half a minute he reappeared and beckoned Ellie in. Looking around the dark, smoky interior, she saw only a man in shirtsleeves who was obviously the alehouse keeper and a middle-aged man drinking ale by the fire. She went over to the hearth to warm herself.

'Ale for both of us,' Philip requested. 'Have you any food?'

The alehouse keeper seemed reluctant to feed them until Philip produced a few coins from a pocket. Obviously relieved to find that the customer was able and willing to pay, the man soon produced bacon and eggs together with some bread. As they attacked the food hungrily he stood by them, anxious to talk.

'I've sent my wife and children to her mother's in Bridgewater,' he told them, 'but I'm not going to abandon everything I own to looters, whether they are rebels or King James' men.'

'Which side do you support?' Philip queried, but the man shook his head.

'Neither — all I want is peace and a chance to earn a living. Joe here feels the same and so do most people.'

The man by the fire nodded.

'Who cares who is called king in London or what religion he is? I'm off to sell a few chickens to whoever will buy them.'

'Off where?'

'Bridgewater. People have to eat, no

matter who wants to rule the country, and I've got some regular customers there.'

'Will you take us with you on your cart?'

The man hesitated and Philip grew persuasive.

'Come on, man! All I want is a ride for myself and my woman! Look at her.' He gestured at Ellie. 'She's been tramping for hours and she is exhausted. Show some pity on her.' He waited for a response, and then said with apparent desperation. 'I'll pay what you owe the landlord.'

The carter grinned, revealing a mouthful of yellow teeth.

'In that case I'll have another mugful of ale.'

In fact it was two more mugfuls and half an hour later before they left the alehouse, after Philip had made a great show of having to hunt through all his pockets to find enough to pay for the carter's drinks. Philip and Ellie climbed into the cart, provoking a flutter of wings and squawks from the chickens penned in a crate. Exhausted, Ellie closed her eyes — then tensed in horror as she felt Philip's arm go around her.

'Relax,' he whispered. 'You are supposed to be my woman, remember? Not long now, and then we will be in Bridgewater and I'll find some gentle-folk to look after us. You have been very brave.'

The unexpected compliment brought tears to her eyes, but she blinked them away and snuggled down in his arms, not stirring until he nudged her awake.

'We are approaching Bridgewater,' he murmured, 'and I don't want to be driven through the centre of the town for everyone to see. There are people with Monmouth who knew me in the Lowlands and I don't want to be recognised.' He raised his voice. 'This is far enough for us, friend.'

The cart halted. Philip leapt off and then helped Ellie down. The carter waved his whip, wished them farewell, and drove on as Ellie looked round. The fields were giving way to houses and market gardens which marked the edge of town.

'This is where we start walking again,' Philip told her, and she groaned.

'How far do you think it is to your friends?'

'A mile — two miles, but no more,' he encouraged her. 'Think of a warm, comfortable bed and hot water to wash yourself.'

'If they will let us in,' she said waspishly, looking at him. With his chin bristling, cropped hair and filthy clothes, he looked the kind of villain that a respectable householder would slam the door on.

'I'll use my charm,' he told her and she laughed reluctantly, and then braced herself as they made their way into town.

The streets were unusually quiet for a midweek afternoon.

'Nobody will venture far from their homes today,' Philip guessed. 'They probably stocked up with food and other necessities yesterday when they heard the latest news, and now they are waiting to see if it is Monmouth or Feversham who comes marching into town before they venture out again.'

He could remember the names and addresses of two men who had been feeding information to him, but he did not know the town and did not want to attract attention to himself. When they saw a rare pedestrian hurrying through the streets it was Ellie who stopped him and asked for directions.

'It's not far,' she reported. 'If we go on and take the next side road on the left we will be there.'

They started to walk faster, anticipating comfort and safety, and soon located the respectable-looking house, but it was ominously silent and there was no response to their knocking. A woman's head appeared in the window of a neighbouring house.

'The Albrights aren't there.'

'When will they be back?'

The woman shook her head. 'They

left in a great hurry two days ago. They said they were going to stay with relatives in Cornwall till all the fuss and fighting settles down.' She looked at them inquisitively.

'Can I give them a message when they come back? Shall I tell them who called?'

Philip thanked the woman, saying there was no need for a message, and led Ellie away from the woman's curiosity. But he was frowning blackly.

'It sounds as though something scared Albright into flight. Maybe he thought he had been betrayed to Monmouth.'

'You mentioned that there were two men here who had been helping you. Where is the other?'

'We heard less from him, but I know his name and that he has an inn somewhere. We'll find it.'

5

They wandered through the streets until they found themselves near the centre of the town. Even here, the streets were virtually empty and many of the shops had their shutters closed. Then the unnatural quiet was suddenly broken by the clatter of hooves as a group of cavalrymen rode rapidly along the main street, led by an elegantly-dressed horseman who was obviously a man of importance. Ellie had a brief glimpse of a proud, pale face as he passed. She turned to find Philip almost crouching in a porch, his face turned away.

'That was Monmouth himself!' he hissed. 'He knows me, and if he had been riding more slowly he would have seen me.'

Ellie gazed with new interest in the direction the horsemen had gone. So that was the rebel leader!

'He is very handsome,' she commented.

'And very vain and foolish.' His hand was resting on the pistol he had thrust into his belt. 'If I could have had one clear shot at him, this uprising would have been over. But if he has been driven back to Bridgewater, then his cause is indeed lost. Let us hope he is not staying in the town, for his men will be in a dangerous mood. We had better find that inn.'

They soon found it, and from the outside it looked a clean and respectable place, though not one of the largest establishments in Bridgewater.

'How do we know if it is safe to go in?' Ellie whispered.

'We don't. We will just have to take a risk.' Philip squared his shoulders. 'It should be quiet at this time of the day, so smile, look as if you hadn't a care in the world, and in we go.'

In fact the inn was empty apart from a middle-aged man cleaning the wooden table tops who looked up sharply as they entered and then managed to raise a welcoming smile.

'How can I help you?'

Philip looked around the room.

'Well, we came in to have a drink and meet people, to find out what the latest news is, but it seems we are out of luck.'

'I'm here. Sit down and I'll bring you some ale.'

He brought a mugful for himself as well and sat down on the adjacent bench.

'Have you just come to Bridgewater? People aren't in the mood for coming out to meet their friends for a gossip these days. Those who could leave Bridgewater have done so, and the rest are in their houses, hoping to God that they will be safe there.'

'And do you feel safe, Master Babcock?' Philip enquired.

The man stared at him in alarm. 'How do you know my name?'

'I've seen your signature on some letters you have been writing to people. My congratulations. You appear to have estimated the number of Monmouth's followers very accurately.'

Master Babcock was pale and wiping the sweat from his brow.

'Are you mad, coming here? The town is full of the Duke's men and they will show no mercy to either of us if they find you or discover that I have been sending your masters information!'

'I'm not here by choice. This young woman and I found ourselves cut off from our friends and have come here looking for your help. We'll leave you in peace as soon as we can.'

The innkeeper sighed.

'There's not much I can do. What do you want?'

'First, a room and some hot water so that my companion can wash and rest, and then perhaps a horse to take us to some quiet spot in Devon where we can lie low for the next few days till the situation is resolved.'

Babcock shook his head.

'A horse? They are in short supply,

and very expensive.'

Philip looked at him impatiently.

'You are an inn-keeper, so either you have horses or know where they can be found. As to money, what price do you put on your life? The sooner we are out of here, the safer you will be.'

The inn-keeper sat silent for a while, tapping his fingers on the table, and then nodded decisively.

'All right. I have a horse I was keeping for myself. You can take it, though if all goes well and you escape safely, I hope you will remember to be grateful in the future. But you'd better wait till dusk. A horse with two strangers will arouse too much interest in the daylight. Meanwhile, I can provide the hot water and a bed.'

He led Ellie upstairs, showed her into a neat bedroom, and brought her a basin of hot water and some coarse towels. Gratefully she washed some of the dust from her face and hands. Just to be in a house under a roof made her feel better. She glanced at the bed, decided she would like a short rest, and was soon fast asleep.

★ ★ ★

Downstairs Philip and the inn-keeper could do little but sit and make idle conversation while they waited for nightfall.

'Why did so many men decide to follow Monmouth?' Philip remarked. 'They must have known he had little hope of success.'

Babcock shrugged.

'I saw him in Taunton, at his so-called 'coronation', with the Taunton Corporation forced to witness the ceremony at sword-point. He is a young, handsome daredevil, the kind to attract followers who have little to lose, and the south-west has suffered hard times in recent years. Besides, this area is strongly Protestant and resented the papist James being imposed upon them as king.'

'They preferred to believe the Duke

when he told them that King Charles had married his mother?'

'It suited them to believe it.'

'But not you?'

'I don't care whether he did or not, I just want to survive, so I chose to support the king. Monmouth has too few experienced soldiers and no hope of reinforcements. It's going to be messy, and bloody, but he will lose, and the sooner the better for all of us.'

They fell silent. Philip settled himself in a quiet corner and fell into a doze, only to be startled awake by the sudden entry of three men. In buff jerkins and heavy boots, with pistols thrust into their belts, they were obviously some of Monmouth's soldiers.

'Ale!' one of them demanded tersely as they threw themselves carelessly on to the nearest benches.

Babcock filled three tankards, which were quickly emptied.

'Again!' A tankard was banged on the table.

Babcock brought the fresh tankards

but remained by the table, and the leader looked up at him impatiently.

'What are you waiting for?'

'Money for the ale,' Babcock said stolidly, and the leader jerked to his feet, and, looking angry, faced the inn-keeper threateningly.

'Money? We come to this God-forsaken place, risking our lives to help free you from the man who calls himself King James and instead of welcoming us as liberators you expect to be paid for a few mugs of ale?' He slammed his fist on the table. 'We'll tell you what we want to drink, you can serve it, and you can forget about asking for money.'

Babcock bit his lip and moved away sullenly. The soldier looked round triumphantly and spotted Philip in his corner.

'You — do you think we should pay?' he challenged him.

Philip stayed silent, pretending to be still half-asleep, and the soldier, sneering, resumed his seat. The three sat drinking sullenly, simply beckoning

Babcock when their tankards were empty, and so an hour or more passed. Then they looked up, alarmed, when they heard the noise of a door shutting. Ellie appeared at the top of the stairs. She hesitated at the sight of the three but decided to continue down and started to cross the room to Philip, ignoring the soldiers. The leader, however, staggered to his feet and grasped her arm.

'Look here, lads! Here's something else to entertain us while we wait for the king's army to arrive!'

'Let me go,' Ellie said furiously, trying to pull away, but now his arm was round her, pulling her to him.

'Don't pretend to be shy. We've got money enough to pay for you.'

'Let her go instantly!'

The command came from Philip, on his feet and with a pistol pointing at the offender. Babcock stooped behind the counter and reappeared holding a hefty cudgel. The man looked from one to another and Ellie tore herself free as the other two soldiers got to their feet uncertainly.

'You dare threaten us? We'll take you to bits!'

The leader fumbled for his pistol but wavered, his brain too befuddled for him to act effectively.

Philip said nothing but his pistol was aimed steadily at the three. He gestured to the inn-keeper.

'Take their weapons.'

Cautiously Babcock approached the soldiers and snatched their pistols.

'Now, leave. You are drunk and stupid, otherwise I'd find your officers and tell them how you are causing trouble among peaceful citizens.'

'We want our weapons!' one of them demanded.

Philip looked at him contemptuously.

'You are leaving with a whole skin, so count yourself lucky.'

They held their ground for a few seconds but then slowly backed out of the inn, the last one shouting a few foul-mouthed insults as soon as he was out of pistol range.

The innkeeper was white and shaking.

'They'll be back! They'll round up their friends and come back to destroy this place! I'm leaving.'

Wide-eyed, Ellie looked at Philip for guidance.

'We have an hour, maybe more,' he said crisply, thrusting his pistol back into his pocket. 'It will take them at least that long to sober up enough to organise a revenge attack. We'll take the horse and whatever provisions you can spare. I assume you know the town well enough to slip away and hide yourself.'

Babcock was already in the private room at the back of the building, throwing open cupboards.

'I started sending information to the king's men because I thought it would help me survive. Now I'm going to lose everything!'

'No!' Philip said urgently. 'These fools may try to wreck your inn, but their officers will soon arrive to whip them off. Monmouth can't afford to alienate the citizens of the town. I give you my word that when this is all over, I will see that you are compensated generously for your losses.'

'If you live,' Ellie heard Babcock mutter. She looked at him in alarm. What would happen to her if she found herself alone in these strange surroundings?

Half an hour later Philip and Ellie were in the inn's stables and he was thrusting bread and cheese into the saddlebags of a thin, worn-out nag that looked as if it would be incapable of more than a slow amble through the streets. Babcock had already vanished into the town's maze of streets.

'Will it carry the two of us?' she asked anxiously.

'It will have to. We have no other choice.'

It looked as though even that choice would be taken from them. Philip's broad back was towards the door, so it was Ellie who first saw the man's figure appear, blocking out the fading light.

'Philip!' she screamed, her hands flying to her face, and he swung round to see the leader of the three soldiers grinning wolvishly at them, his pistol aimed.

'Running away?' the man mocked. 'You should have been quicker.'

He fired, but the flintlock pistol hung fire for a precious instant that gave Philip the chance to throw himself aside before the gun exploded. Ellie, looking round desperately, seized an old horse-shoe and hurled it at the soldier. It hit him hard on the forehead and he dropped to the ground. Philip ran towards him, picked up the pistol, and then checked the man.

'Have I killed him?' Ellie whispered.

'Unfortunately, no, but he won't wake up for quite a while.' Philip stood listening hard for some seconds. 'I can't hear anyone else. He must have come back by himself, but his friends won't be far behind him.' He crossed back to the horse, unhitched it, and swung himself into the saddle. 'Mount! We've got to leave here now.'

He stretched his right arm down and pulled Ellie up so she sat behind him, and then he urged the horse into movement. It seemed reluctant to leave the comfort of its stable at first but Philip kicked it into action.

'It may be slow, but we don't want to attract attention by galloping through town,' he muttered, glancing round the quiet streets. There was no sound of pursuit and no one seemed to notice them as they made their way out of town. Ellie's thumping heart steadied. They seemed to be making a successful escape.

Half an hour later and they had left the outskirts of the town behind them. Ellie looked back as the last lighted windows faded from view and breathed a deep sigh of relief. She tightened her grip round Philip's waist, glad now of the warmth of his body.

'Don't crush me!' he said harshly. 'Let me breathe.'

She loosened her hold. Freed from worries of armed pursuit, she began to brood again on the future. Bridgewater had failed to give them a safe haven. How long would it take them to reach somewhere free from Monmouth's men, and how would they find someone willing to shelter them till danger was past? And suppose Philip was wrong, and Monmouth triumphed against all the odds? What would happen to them then?

She was roused from her thoughts when Philip suddenly reined in the horse.

'What's the matter?'

He pointed to where a gleam of moonlight through the ragged clouds showed a small building a little way off the path. There were no lights visible.

'We are going to see whether there is anyone in. If not, we will spend the night there.'

'But can't the horse go further? It doesn't seem to be in any distress!'

Philip ignored her and turned towards the building. As they neared it he slipped from the saddle and led the horse up to the rough door which he pushed open. He went in and Ellie heard flint strike steel and saw the flare of a small flame, and then Philip came out.

'It's empty. Whoever lived here has obviously abandoned it,' he reported and held his right hand out to help Ellie from the horse. He unbuckled the saddle bags, picked one up, again using his right hand and gestured at the other bag. 'You can bring that if you don't mind.'

She dragged the heavy bag along the ground and through the door after him, and found herself in a one-roomed windowless hovel. It contained a pile of bracken covered with a blanket which had obviously served the occupant as a bed and two rough stools in front of a fireplace. Philip had found a stub of tallow candle which now flickered on the hearth, deepening shadows in the corners.

'It will have to do,' Philip said tersely as he saw her look of distaste. Then he strode outside back to the horse and struck it hard on its hindquarters. The horse neighed indignantly but did not move. Once more Philip's hand fell, and then again, and finally the terrified horse bolted, galloping off into the darkness and leaving the pair of them with no means of escape from this bleak shelter.

'What are you doing? Have you gone mad?' Ellie shouted desperately at Philip, but he did not seem to hear her. Slowly he came back and stood holding on to the doorframe with one hand.

'What's wrong with you?' she demanded, but instead of answering he closed his eyes and slid very gently downwards until he was sitting on the floor. She stared at him and he managed to look up and give a twisted grin.

'Help me to the bed, Ellie — please.'

She bent, slipped her arm around him and half-lifted him. With her help he shuffled to the rough bed, where he collapsed, apparently unconscious. When she took her hand away it felt wet and the candlelight showed a dark stain on her fingers. Horrified, Ellie turned Philip on his back and opened his coat and waistcoat. When she brought the candle over to him, she could see that the left side of his shirt and his waistcoat were soaked with blood.

His eyelids flickered and he looked up at her.

'I thought the shot missed,' she said blankly. 'Why didn't you tell me?'

'There was no point. We had to get away before his friends came,' Philip murmured. 'Don't look so horrified. It hit my left shoulder, nothing vital, but I've lost quite a bit of blood, I think, and that has made me too weak to go any further tonight. It is a pity you didn't throw that horseshoe earlier.'

'Why did you drive the horse away?'

'If we are followed, with luck they will search for the horse, not two fugitives in a den like this.' He winced with pain.

'What can I do to help?' Ellie asked practically.

He glanced down at his stained shirt.

'You can get this sodden mess off me and then tear up the clean bits and use them to staunch the blood.' There was a faint smile. 'And if you look in the saddlebags you will find a bottle of brandy. I could do with a drink.'

She found the bottle and he tipped the neck up to his mouth greedily. Gently Ellie eased off his coat, waistcoat and shirt. After a brief inspection of the ruined shirt she threw it into a corner, turned away and lifted her skirt, took off a petticoat and tore it into strips. In a few minutes she had contrived a pad for the wound and secured it in place with bandages. Philip, gripped by a sudden shivering fit, nodded wordless thanks. Hastily she pulled off his boots and tucked his coat round him.

'I saw some logs piled outside. Shall I try to start a fire?' she asked, but he shook his head urgently.

'We can't risk any pursuers seeing the light of a fire or smoke from the chimney.'

'Then we will have to keep each other warm,' she said resolutely.

She contrived a supper of bread and cheese for herself, and swallowed a warming mouthful of brandy, and though Philip refused the food he had another drink of brandy. Then she snuffed out the candle and lay down, once again, beside him.

6

Time passed. Ellie was exhausted but could not sleep and she knew from his breathing that Philip was still awake. Then another shivering fit shook him and she moved closer, putting her arm round him as if to comfort a child.

'That's good, thank you,' Philip murmured.

She could feel the warmth from his body as it curved snugly against hers. This must be what it was like to share a marriage bed.

There was silence for a while, though she could tell from his breathing that he was still awake. He stirred.

'Elgiva,' he said drowsily. 'I still can't understand a father who calls his daughter Elgiva and also gives his permission for her to marry a man whom he has never met.'

Ellie sighed resignedly.

'As I told you, all my father has ever really cared about is the early history of England and his family's possible links with its kings. My father once said that I was lucky to bear the name of a famous queen.'

'But history was not his only interest always. After all, he did marry your mother, did he not?'

'I believe she was very pretty, and he was distracted by her, but only for a short time. He once said that his marriage had been an aberration, and I doubt if he mourned my mother when she died. Her passing meant he was free once again to devote all his energies to his historical research.'

'Yet he had you.'

'Very rarely. I was farmed out to various friends as a baby. Then Lady Pontin virtually adopted me as a sister for Mary, and apart from an occasional payment for my expenses and pin money he was able to forget me completely.'

'How do you think he will react when

he finds you are now a rich woman?'

She was silent for a while, and then said hesitantly, 'I think his reaction will be pleasure, that he will now have more to spend on documents and research.' Her voice grew stronger. 'And then I will tell him that the money is mine, and that I intend to spend it on myself to make up for all his years of neglect!'

She felt Philip quiver with laughter.

'Do you think that is wrong? That it is undutiful and selfish?'

'No!' he returned emphatically. 'Stick to your resolve. I just wish I could be there when you face him.'

'Was your childhood very different?'

'Very. I was lucky. My parents loved me as well as each other. When my father was killed out hunting ten years ago, my mother mourned him deeply. Now she spends her time urging me to marry and give her grandchildren.'

Finally, reluctantly, sleep came to them.

★ ★ ★

Ellie woke, wondering at first where she was. Philip stirred uneasily as she carefully slipped away from him and felt her way to the door. Outside it was a grey, damp dawn, but she was relieved to see that there was a small stream nearby. At least there would be fresh water for drinking and washing. She splashed her face, shuddering at the cold. When she re-entered she found that the draught from the door had roused Philip. He blinked up at her groggily.

'Is everything all right?'

'I have looked very carefully, but I cannot see another living soul, and I have found that we have water to drink as well as brandy.'

He licked his lips.

'I am certainly thirsty.'

She had noticed a couple of rough pottery bowls abandoned on a make-shift shelf and now she took one, filled it at the stream, and brought it back to him. He drank gratefully. In spite of the cold air pouring into the hut he threw his coat aside, complaining that it was too warm. He was flushed and his forehead was hot to the touch. Ellie felt helpless. How could she deal with a fever with no medicines and no hope of summoning a doctor? As gently as possible she removed the dressing from his wound. It was no longer bleeding but looked red and inflamed, which worried her further as she rebandaged it and saw how Philip was biting his lip at the pain. When she had finished he lay exhausted for some time, then struggled to sit up.

'Lie down, rest,' she told him, but he shook his head.

'Ellie, listen. Do you know how to fire a pistol?'

She nodded.

'Good. We have my pistol and the one I took from the soldier. If I get worse . . . ' She started to protest at such talk, but angrily he waved her to silence. 'If I get worse, take one pistol and leave the other with me. Follow the track but avoid people if you can. You must come to a town or village eventually. Go to the church, find the minister and tell him your story. Ask for shelter.'

'You are going to recover, and we shall go on together!'

He gripped her wrist. 'Promise me you will do what I say!'

To pacify him she nodded reluctantly and he released her and sank back.

She broke her fast with cheese and stale bread, but Philip wanted nothing but water. She sat on a stool and watched him anxiously as the day passed slowly and he lay half-asleep and restive. Some time after noon she realised that he was awake and looking at her steadily.

'You feel better!' she exclaimed with relief, but he shook his head.

'I am growing weaker. There is no way I can leave here with you. Take the pistol and go now.'

'I can't leave you here, all alone, wounded! What will you do without me?'

Even as she spoke the answer came to her.

'You will kill yourself. That is why you want me to leave you the other pistol.'

Stern and determined, he did not deny it.

'Would you rather that I died slowly, out of my mind with fever? All I can do now is send you away to find safety. Now go — please, Ellie.'

Sobbing, she knelt by the bed and gathered his head to her breast.

'I will not leave you to die alone!'

Suddenly Ellie felt him tense and pull away at the same time as she became aware that the light from the doorway had been cut off. She scrambled to her feet and saw the dark outline of a man with another behind him and as the man advanced into the hovel she saw the naked sword held steadily in his right hand. Desperately Philip reached for the pistol which lay by the bed, but the man took two fast steps and kicked the weapon out of his reach.

The newcomer was a man in his forties, roughly but serviceably dressed, with a grim, unshaven face. The other figure, now venturing uncertainly into the interior, was a youth of about fifteen, tall and gangly, who stared first at Philip and then at Ellie.

'What'll we do, Uncle Jem?' the boy asked uncertainly. 'Can we stay here?'

The man did not reply. Instead he gazed at Philip and Ellie as if noting everything about them, and then picked up Philip's coat and examined it carefully before dropping it back on the bed. Only then did he speak.

'Look at their clothes, Davey. They may be dirty and torn but they are fine quality. We've got the gentry here.' His gaze rested on Philip. 'But the gentleman is wounded. I reckon we have a pair of fugitives looking for a place to hide, just like us.' Abruptly he thrust his sword into his belt. 'We can stay here, Davey.' He turned towards Ellie. 'Just so long as the lady stops trying to edge over towards that pistol.'

Ellie stopped her slow sideways movement. Defiantly she confronted the man.

'You are right to some extent. This gentleman and I are your betters and we were here first, so will you please leave!'

The man grinned at her with amusement.

'My lady, I wish we could, but the rain is threatening and the lad and I need shelter. Now, suppose we see if we can help each other.' He turned to the youth. 'Davey, bring in some of those logs and we'll get a fire going.'

'No!' exclaimed Ellie. 'What about the smoke?'

Jem glanced at her sideways.

'I doubt if there is anyone within five miles of this God-forsaken spot at the moment, and when it starts raining the smoke won't be visible for any distance. Anyway, we need a fire.'

Davey brought in armfuls of wood and with flint and tinder Jem started a small blaze which gradually grew and seized on the logs. A helpless onlooker, Ellie still responded gratefully to the light and the warmth. Jem turned to her.

'Do you have any food?'

'Some cheese and dry bread,' she admitted reluctantly.

Jem shook his head, unimpressed. 'Let's hope we can do better than that.'

He clapped the boy on the back.

'Davey, someone lived here and they can't have taken everything with them. Do your best and see what you can find.'

The boy vanished obediently and returned some time later with a wide smile. He held out his hands, displaying four eggs.

'There are two chickens running wild. I found their nests and I've got their eggs, Uncle Jem. Should I kill the birds if I can catch them?'

The man shook his head.

'Not yet. Let them lay some more eggs.'

Soon he was busy over the fire. Philip and Ellie watched as he boiled water in one of the pots and then slipped the eggs in with quick, economical movements. He saw them watching and grinned.

'A bachelor has to master some skills if he's not to starve. Now, mistress, give me that stale bread you talked about.'

Ellie suddenly felt extremely hungry and wondered whether they would have to sit and watch the newcomers eat, but Jem shared out the boiled eggs with bread softened in the water together with the remaining cheese. Even Philip ate a little. Jem carefully ate the last scrap of bread and sighed.

'We haven't eaten for more than a day. That was a feast.' He turned to Philip and looked at him appraisingly.

'Now, in return for your bread and cheese, let's take a look at you and see if we can help.'

All Ellie's fears returned. 'Don't touch him! We don't know who you are. Are you for Monmouth or the king?'

Jem knelt by Philip and looked up at her.

'Does it matter? Your man needs

help. We'll talk about loyalties later.'

Gently he exposed the wound. Philip gasped with pain as Jem prodded the area around it and then nodded.

'The ball is still in there. At least I can get that out.'

★ ★ ★

The next half hour was an endurance test. Jem cleaned his pocket knife in the hot water he had used for the eggs and then beckoned Ellie and Davey.

'He'll fight. You two must hold him down.'

Ellie felt the tension in Philip's body and then, as the knife penetrated the wound he screamed in agony and tried to twist away while Ellie and Davey held him as still as they could. Ellie realised that tears were running down her face. The youth looked across at her and tried to offer encouragement.

'Uncle Jem knows what he's doing, honestly. He's often treated people in our village.'

In fact a wicked, blood-covered little ball of lead was soon extracted. As it lay in the palm of his hand, Jem looked down at Philip.

'Can you take a little more?'

Philip nodded. Ellie saw that he had bitten his lower lip till it bled. He closed his eyes, white and sweating, while Jem swabbed the wound with the hot water and finished by pouring the last dregs of the brandy into it. Philip groaned and lapsed into merciful unconsciousness while Jem rapidly used up the last of the bandages.

'Well, that may have helped,' Jem said philosophically. 'At least the ball is out and the wound is cleaner.'

'Will he recover?' Ellie whispered.

'I've seen worse get better. You'll just have to wait.'

With the fire burning and four of them crowded in the small hut, the atmosphere grew stifling, but when the door was opened the cold wet blast of the wind made them cower.

'Davey,' Jem said after a while when

the boy's fidgeting was beginning to
fret Ellie, 'you may be able to find more
to eat somewhere nearby. The rain is
easing off, so why don't you go and
look?' He turned to Ellie. 'Perhaps you
could help him, mistress.'

It was worded as a suggestion but
sounded like a gentle command and
Ellie found herself deciding that she
would like a breath of fresh air, so
she wrapped Philip's cloak around her
and followed Davey. First he proudly
showed her the hens' nests hidden in
the grass and they collected two more
eggs. Then they discovered there was
a small vegetable patch behind the
cottage with a few straggly plants
surviving in it.

'There are some little carrots and a
few onions,' Davey said, surveying it.

'What are those plants?'

'Herbs,' he told her. 'Mint and
marjoram, mostly. I look after our
garden at home and I grow them for my
mother.'

Lacking tools, they resorted to

digging the vegetables up with their bare hands. While they were making sure that they had not missed any, Davey glanced at Ellie shyly.

'You and that gentleman belong to the king's party, don't you? Uncle Jem said none of the gentry were supporting the Duke of Monmouth.'

Ellie squatted back on her heels.

'We support the rightful king,' she said firmly. 'What made you follow the bastard duke?'

'He's not a bastard!' Davey said hotly, and then blushed. 'At least, he says he's not.' He shrugged. 'Anyway, when the fine horsemen came to our village and asked us to fight for the real king of England, we didn't take much persuading. We've had hard times recently, we don't want a Papist on the throne — and we thought it'd be exciting, glorious even — different to our ordinary lives.'

He stopped abruptly.

'But it wasn't?' Ellie said sadly, and he shook his head emphatically.

'Uncle Jem said it would be hard work and misery. He didn't want to go with the soldiers, but my father was his brother and Uncle Jem promised him that he would look after me and my mother, years ago when my father took sick and died. She begged him to go with me and try to keep me safe. We set off marching with a drummer to lead us, but it wasn't exciting. The weather turned cold and we soon ate the food we'd brought with us and nobody gave us any more. The gentry shut their gates on us and threatened to shoot us. We were hungry, most of us hadn't any weapons and nobody seemed to know what we were supposed to be doing.'

'Then we met a group of the king's soldiers and we fought them as best we could. There were more of us so they soon ran away, but some men were killed.' His face was heavy with memories. 'It wasn't glorious. It was frightening, and not all the men died quickly. My friend Peter, he died in agony and I could do nothing to help

116

him. Next we heard that the king's men had reached Bristol before us and that's when Jem told me the Duke had lost all chance of winning and that he was taking me home. We slipped away in the middle of the night, but we've had to avoid Monmouth's men as well as the king's, and we're still a long way from home.'

Ellie reached out and patted his arm comfortingly.

'We all want to go home, and it doesn't matter whether you are for the king or Monmouth, we'll help each other.'

He managed a smile, and they rinsed the vegetables in the stream and went back to the others. Jem and Philip were deep in conversation when they returned and she gathered that the two men had been explaining to each other what had brought them to their present situation.

'Jem says that the last news they heard was that Monmouth was retreating, but was pinned down near Bridgewater,' Philip told her.

Jem made use of his cooking skills again to concoct a rather watery cross between a vegetable soup and a stew, but at least it was warming and stopped them feeling too hungry. Philip was very weak but Ellie spooned a little into his mouth.

'It looks as if it will be chicken tomorrow,' Jem said as he drained the cooking bowl.

Ellie spent the night once again huddled up to Philip, while Jem and Davey took it in turns to stand guard and sleep. Jem's snores unfortunately did not make sleep any easier.

★　★　★

The next day dawned with watery sunshine. The hens had produced more eggs and were therefore given a temporary reprieve. Philip was still very weak but at least there was no more fever.

At midmorning Davey was exploring the land around the cottage and Ellie was standing outside with her face turned up to the comforting sun when she became aware that Jem had come outside to stand beside her.

'The weather is improving,' he commented, 'and Davey and I have had a good rest so we'll probably be off today.'

Ellie looked at him, startled. In less than twenty-four hours he had become a friend. What would they do without him and his skills? He had more to say.

'I've had a talk with your man. He's asked me if we'll take you with us when we leave here. I'm agreeable enough to that, but what do you say, mistress?'

She could not answer at once — after all, she might be choosing between life and death — but finally she shook her head.

'Thank you, Jem, but I must stay with Philip. I am the reason he is in this situation, and I must stay with him and do what I can for him. The fever has gone, thanks to you getting the pistol ball out. If I can feed him on eggs and herbs, and possibly a chicken, perhaps he will get strong enough soon for us to make our way to some town.'

Jem shrugged. 'I told him that is what you would say. Well, without a doubt you are a brave and loyal lass, but if you decide to come with us after all when I decide it is time for us to go, I swear I shall understand.'

Ellie went back into the cottage.

'I am not going with them,' she told Philip without preamble. 'I was your responsibility — now you are mine. I am going to stay here and I'll feed you up with chicken soup until you are fit to leave with me.'

He stretched out and took her hand.

'A few days ago I thought you were a silly child, but now I know that you are a brave woman. You have put up with hardship and danger without complaint. If we get out of this alive, we will have cause to be grateful to each other.'

7

Davey was calling urgently. 'Uncle Jem! Uncle Jem!' Ellie ran out to see what was the matter and almost collided with the boy as he rushed towards the hut seeking his uncle.

'Uncle Jem, there's a man coming this way!'

His uncle placed a hand on his shoulder.

'Steady, boy! Do you mean he is coming along the track or is he making for this cottage? Is he on horseback?'

Davey shook his head.

'He's on foot, but he's coming across the heath and he keeps stopping and looking around. I crouched down and then crawled away so he didn't see me.'

'Well done, Davey. Leave the rest to me. Take Mistress Ellie into the cottage, smother the fire, and don't make a noise.'

They moved quickly to obey him. Ellie told Philip what Davey had seen. They waited silently until Jem stepped through the door.

'From the way he is behaving, it is a man on the run from danger, and he is probably making for this cottage.' He picked up his sword from where he had discarded it beside the hearth. 'I'll hide behind the cottage till he reaches the door. Mistress Ellie, you take a pistol and wait just inside by the door.' There was a protest from Davey. 'No, Davey, I want you free to tackle him and make him prisoner, so you can stand on the other side of the doorway.'

They were soon in position, waiting tensely. Time seemed to stand still, but Ellie thought about ten minutes had probably passed when they heard heavy footsteps and a man's rough, gasping breaths. He paused outside the door and then thrust it open. At the same time those inside heard Jem's challenge and a split second later a figure dived headlong through the door. Ellie did not have to use the pistol because Davey was on the man instantly, pinning him to the ground. Jem came in and pointed his pistol at the captive.

'Sit up! Let's see who you are!' he commanded harshly.

The man sat up, with Davey holding his arms behind him. He was in his thirties — haggard and wild-eyed. A sash across his jerkin suggested that he had belonged to some military force, but he was unarmed as far as they could see.

'Don't shoot me!' he begged. 'I was just looking for food. Have you any to spare? I am starving. All I want to do is go home!'

Jem bent forward and patted the man over to make sure there were no hidden weapons, then gestured to Davey to release him.

'We all seem to have the same wish. We all want to get home safely.' He poured some of his latest cooking, a mess of vegetables, into a bowl which he gave to the man who devoured it eagerly. When he had finished, Jem continued the interrogation.

'What are you running from?'

The man lowered the bowl and stared at him.

'Haven't you heard? The Duke of Monmouth has been defeated at Sedgemoor and the king's men are hunting his followers down like rats!'

There was a moment's profound silence. Philip, propped on one elbow, broke it.

'Tell us all you know!'

'We were near Sedgemoor. There weren't enough of us left following the duke to face the king's army in a pitched battle, so he decided to try a surprise night attack. But we didn't know what we were doing. The king's men withstood our onslaught and then counter-attacked. They had artillery — we didn't. Their cavalry broke through our centre and scattered us. I know hundreds died then and they are chasing the rest of us.'

'Was the Duke of Monmouth killed?'

'I don't know, but I don't think so.' He looked up hopefully. 'Is there any more food? We were hungry before the battle began, and I haven't eaten since.'

Jem gave him some more of the vegetable stew before crossing to sit by Philip and consult him quietly. Finally he stood up, hands on hips, and sighed.

'Well, this news alters things. Davey and I thought we could take our time, making our way home quietly bit by bit, but with King James's troopers combing the land we haven't got that choice. We will have to leave at once before they find us here.' He looked at the fugitive resignedly. 'You are welcome to come with us. We can help each other.'

The man nodded eagerly and Jem turned to Ellie.

'At least this is good news for you', he said. 'Our enemies are your friends. You can stay here now in safety and wait for them to find you.'

Philip was nodding his agreement.

'Go — and good luck. You have saved my life and if I can do anything for you in the future I will, but if we are all found together I doubt if I will be given time to explain before they slaughter the lot of us.'

It took only a few minutes for the little party to be ready to leave. Davey gave Ellie a shy smile but Jem hugged her roughly.

'Look after him. You make a good couple.'

Then he beckoned to the stranger and strode out of the hut. Ellie stood at the door and watched their figures slowly dwindle in the distance. She felt as if she had said goodbye to old friends.

When she went indoors, Philip was sitting propped against the wall.

'From what the man said, the troopers should be here by nightfall. Look out for them and when you see them wave and shout and make it clear you are trying to attract their attention. Fugitives would try to hide. We must show we want them to find us. Now, where are my boots?'

He found them, tried to thrust his right foot into one and looked impatiently at Ellie. 'You'll have to help me pull them on.'

'What are you doing? You're still too weak to get up!'

'Ellie, I am not going to let our rescuers find me sprawled on a pile of hay like a landed fish. I have some dignity!'

Reluctantly she bent to help him pull on his boots, but was suddenly overcome by hysterical laughter. Philip stared at her in bewilderment.

'I'm sorry! But a few days ago I hardly dared speak to the great Earl of Arlbury. Now I am helping you dress!'

'After feeding me, keeping me warm at night, and tearing up your petticoats to make bandages for me!' He laughed. 'Well, my girl, once we are back in civilised surroundings you had better show me more respect! Now, make me look my best.'

His shirt was gone, of course, but he straightened his waistcoat and she helped him gingerly into his coat.

'How do I look?' he asked.

'You look like a scarecrow ready to collapse at any moment.'

'Thank you very much. I can't say you look much better.'

They scowled at each other and then, suddenly, Philip hugged her. For a second they took comfort in each other's nearness. The worst was over. Rescue was coming and soon they would return to normal life.

★ ★ ★

Ellie saw the troopers as soon as she stepped outside. There were half a dozen of them, riding fast, and they saw Ellie before she could raise a hand to summon them. She heard a shout and saw them change direction, riding towards her. She dived back into the cottage.

'They're here!' she said breathlessly.

Philip was upright, though leaning against the wall for support. Horses' hooves thudded outside the door, there was a shouted command, and then the troopers came in — but not, it was immediately apparent, as rescuers. The leader's sword was in his hand. He glanced round, and then nodded at Philip.

'Take him,' he said to the two soldiers who followed him. They strode across the floor and seized Philip's arms. He shouted with pain and swayed dizzily. Ellie ran towards them.

'Stop! He is Lord Arlbury, one of King James's advisors!' She turned to the officer. 'He is wounded and needs your help.'

The man laughed openly at her. 'A fine lie from a rebel! Can you prove this man is a lord and a supporter of the king?'

Philip and Ellie looked at each other blankly. The only proof they had was their word. The soldier sneered, taking their silence as an admission of their falsehood.

'Take me to your headquarters,' Philip said tersely. 'There will be people there who will know me.'

The man shook his head dismissively.

'I haven't the time to waste. You are wounded and in hiding. Obviously you are one of Monmouth's men and you will soon get your just deserts.' He poked his head out of the door. 'Can you see the cart yet?' he asked someone, listened to the reply, and turned back to Philip.

'You are lucky. You're going to get a ride to your place of execution.'

'No!' Ellie screamed. 'Listen to us! I can tell you things that will convince you I am telling the truth.'

'I'm sure you would spin a fine tale,' he said, and beckoned to the two men holding Philip. 'Bring him out.'

Ellie clutched at his arm and he swore, throwing her off him so that she fell heavily to the ground while Philip was half-dragged, half-carried outside. She leapt up and followed. A rough cart driven by two men was approaching along the nearby track. As it came near she could see that it held half a dozen men huddled together, their hands and feet tied. One of the drivers held a musket.

'Here's another rebel for you,' the officer announced. 'Put him in the cart with the others.' Philip's captors pushed him roughly into the cart, tying him like the other prisoners with lengths of rope which the drivers produced.

The troopers swung themselves back on their horses.

'Maybe we'll find a few more before dark,' the officer said, turning his horse's head to lead his men away.

'What about me?' said Ellie, panicking. 'You can't leave me here. Let me go with him.' She looked at him beseechingly. What else could she do?

The officer looked at her, hesitated, and then shrugged.

'Why not? If you want to see your man die.'

Ellie scrambled into the cart and made herself a small space beside Philip. The cart set off, jolting over the track. Philip was barely conscious. The rough handling had obviously been too much in his weakened state and Ellie put her arm round him to cushion him as far as she could.

The other captives said nothing but sat with their heads bowed. A couple wore bloodied bandages. All looked weary and dispirited.

After some time they came to a cluster of houses. The guard with the musket got down and swaggered up to the door of the nearest cottage and banged on it with his fist. When it opened he shouldered his way in and emerged a few minutes later clutching some food which he prepared to share with the driver. Ellie suddenly realised how hungry she was.

'Aren't you going to feed these men?' she asked indignantly, and was laughed at once more.

'What's the point of feeding them? They'll all be dead by nightfall,' the guard told her.

'At least let me get them some water,' she argued.

'Water?' He shrugged. 'Why not? You can have a few minutes while we eat our food anyway.'

Ellie slipped from the cart and ran to the cottage. When she knocked it was opened by a man, probably in his fifties, who looked at her in despair.

'What is it now? You've taken our food and we'll go hungry to bed tonight.'

'Please, give me water for those poor men,' Ellie begged him.

He looked at the cart and then sighed. 'Poor souls!'

With Ellie's help he filled a bucket with fresh water and produced two tankards which he and Ellie filled and then held to the mouth of each of the thirsty men in turn. Finally Ellie drank deep. There were tears in her eyes, but her thanks to the cottager were cut short by the driver warning her that he was about to drive on and she hurriedly took her place beside Philip.

As the cart trundled on Philip turned his head and whispered in her ear.

'You must get away! I've seen the way that men who've been fighting and won treat a defenceless woman. The next time we stop, run away and hide.' She nodded, but he gripped her arm fiercely. 'This time, woman, do as you are told!'

But the cart did not stop again until it rumbled into Taunton. Here the king's soldiers were everywhere. The drivers greeted some of them as old friends and followed their directions to a town square, which normally would have been used as a market place but which was now full of foot soldiers, cavalry, and a group of prisoners under guard.

One of the drivers saw an officer and called out to him.

'Sir, we have brought more prisoners. Where shall we take them?'

The officer looked at him impatiently.

'Take them? We've nowhere for you to take them. We have too many prisoners as it is.' He pointed to the sullen group of prisoners standing nearby. 'Why don't you follow them?'

'Where are they going, sir?'

'To be hanged,' came the answer. 'They will all hang soon anyway, so there is no point in wasting time listening to their lies and excuses.'

Ellie froze, and then leapt from the cart to confront him.

'You can't hang them like that! This is Lord Arlbury, one of King James's most trusted counsellors!'

The officer ignored her and walked away, but her voice had made one of the prisoners in the group look up.

'Mistress Ellie! It's me, Davey, and Uncle Jem!'

It was indeed the pair who had helped them so much. Davey's face was bruised and there was blood on Jem's jerkin, but he nodded to Ellie.

'The troopers killed the other man,' Davey confided in a low voice. 'One was going to kill me but Uncle Jem pulled him off his horse and killed him with his own sword.'

One of their guards prodded Davey with his musket.

'Quiet! We shall be moving off in a minute, and you'll be swinging from the gallows within the hour.'

Ellie looked round desperately. How could she help Philip? Daylight was already fading, but all she could see were prisoners and armed men. There was an inn on one side of the square which seemed to be the centre of activity, and as she looked towards it a small group of gentlemen came out and stood conferring on the steps. She stared, gasped, then gathered up her skirts and ran towards the inn, but when she was still some distance away guards thrust up their muskets to form a barrier.

'You can't come through here! Get back to you friends!' she was commanded.

'Let me through! One of my friends is there!' she entreated, almost weeping with frustration, but the muskets were not lowered. Ellie took a step backwards and filled her lungs.

'Daniel, it's me, Ellie! Help me!' The men on the steps did not seem to hear her above the hubbub of activity. She tried again. 'Daniel! It's Ellie, Mary's friend! Please, help!'

She threw herself at the guards, trying to break through, screaming and hitting out at them, but they thrust her back easily.

Then, as she stood panting with desperate tears running down her face, Daniel's head turned and he slowly scanned the crowd as if looking for the source of the disturbance. His gaze passed over her, then returned as she waved wildly at him. Then he was striding rapidly towards her. As the guards finally lowered their muskets he looked at her with incredulity and then stretched out his arms and she fell into them, sobbing with relief.

'Ellie? Where have you been?' He looked around. 'Is Arlbury with you?'

Ellie swung round to point to the cart which held Arlbury, and saw that it had gone, together with the small group of prisoners. She swayed. No! This couldn't happen just when help was at hand!

'They are taking him to be hanged,' she whispered. 'He was in a cart just there a moment ago, but it has gone.'

Daniel seized her hand and pulled her through the crowd to the officer who had given instruction to the drivers.

'There was a cart here. Where is it?' he demanded.

The officer pointed casually up a street and Daniel hurried in that direction, followed by Ellie. It did not take long to catch up with the cart and the prisoners and Daniel's air of authority was enough to halt the little procession when he ordered the guards to stop. Ellie clambered up the side of the cart.

'Look, Daniel, here's Philip. He's alive but wounded.'

Daniel's face was full of horror. Philip, huddled in the cart, managed to raise a kind of smile, a grimace.

'You are just in time, Danbury. I am exceedingly glad to see you.'

Urgently Daniel beckoned a passing

horseman and ordered him to dismount and assist him, and then the two of them gently lifted Philip out of the cart. When the horseman had remounted Daniel helped him take Philip up in his arms.

'Carry him to the inn. Tell them there that he is the Earl of Arlbury and get him a doctor at once,' Daniel ordered, and then turned to Ellie. 'My dear, we must get you food and shelter, and some fresh clothes as well. Afterwards you can tell me your story.'

But Ellie had become aware of a man staring at her with desperate entreaty. It was Jem, and as he caught her eye he nodded beseechingly at Davey. Ellie grasped Daniel's arm.

'There are two other prisoners — they helped us. Philip would have died without them. Can we save them?'

'Which are they?'

She led him to them.

'This is Jem and his nephew Davey.'

Daniel turned to the man leading the guards.

'I will take responsibility for these two.'

The man was shaking his head.

'Not the older man, you don't, who-ever you are. He killed one of my friends and he is going to hang before nightfall.'

Daniel looked at him sharply and saw that he was adamant.

'What about the boy?'

The guard shrugged. 'Oh, you can take the boy if you like.'

Davey stood blank-faced, wondering what was happening, until Ellie took him gently by the hand.

'You are coming with us now,' she said softly. 'We'll take you back home, to your mother.'

She looked back to Jem with despair, but he squared his shoulders and smiled bravely at her.

'Tell his mother I did my best,' he instructed her. 'Thank you, mistress. God be with you.'

Then the guards' leader shouted a command and the little group resumed their march towards the fate that awaited them.

8

Ellie's overwhelming feeling was of relief. Philip was safe. She was safe. Now it was Daniel's responsibility, not hers, to look after them and make decisions about their future.

Daniel escorted her back to the inn where they found his crisp instructions had been rapidly carried out. Philip had already been installed in a bedroom and a doctor was with him. Davey was entrusted to the care of Daniel's escort and after some argument with the harassed landlord a small attic bedroom was cleared for Ellie.

'Do you require food or a wash first?' Daniel asked her kindly as she stood swaying with fatigue.

'Food, please!'

She ate greedily. It had only been a few days in fact since she had last eaten a proper meal on a plate, at a table, but it felt as if it had been years. Finally she pushed her empty dish away and smiled at Daniel apologetically.

'I should have asked before. How is Mary?'

'Frantic with worry about you. She blames herself for running away.'

'She had cause to be frightened.' A memory came back. 'We saw flames rising from Danbury! What happened?'

'More marauders — a large gang. They burnt some outbuildings and the stable block but we fought them off and the house itself is undamaged. Now I shall order hot water and clean towels to be put in your room.'

She smiled. 'I gather you think I really need a wash.'

He smiled back. 'Actually, Ellie, you really do.'

However, when he returned she was fast asleep with her head resting on the table. He looked at her for a while, marvelling how the quiet, neat young girl he remembered had become this ragged woman who forgot all about dignity and proper behaviour and fought to save her friends. Finally he picked her up, carried her to her room, and instructed a maid to take off her shoes and stockings and cover her with blankets.

*   *   *

When Ellie woke the next morning she lay for a few minutes luxuriating in the simple pleasure of a bed with a comfortable mattress which didn't rustle when she moved. Then she climbed out of bed, looked round, and found herself confronting a dirty, untidy scarecrow. She examined her reflection in the mirror and groaned. Like Daniel she was amazed at her transformation but she was eager to restore her image to that of Mistress Elgiva Colinridge, a lady of gentle birth — and, she remembered suddenly, of considerable wealth.

There was a hesitant tap on the door, which opened slowly to reveal two maids, one carrying a basin, soap and linen towels, and the other a large jug of hot water. They deposited their burdens and scuttled out while Ellie thankfully shed the remains of the clothes she had been wearing since she left Danbury and began to wash herself.

Restored to comparative cleanliness, she was wondering whether she could bear to don her rags once more when there was another, firmer knock and a large woman whom she recognised from the evening before as the landlord's wife entered, her arms full of clothes.

'I think my daughter and you are near enough in size,' she announced, laying the clothes on the bed. 'And we've brought you some breakfast as well.'

A maid half-hidden by her mistress's bulk was holding a covered tray which she put down carefully on a side table before following her mistress out of the room.

Clean, decently clothed and well-fed!

Ellie made her way downstairs half an hour later absolutely delighted with life. Daniel was waiting for her and eyed her transformation appreciatively.

'Now you look like the Ellie I know,' he approved.

'I feel more like her. How is Philip — Lord Arlbury?'

'He has spent a comfortable night. The physician says he is weak from loss of blood and rough handling but the wound is clean and healing. I have requisitioned a travelling coach from a gentleman who seems eager to please. Actually, I think in return he want us to overlook any support he may have given the rebel Monmouth. A mattress and blankets have been put in it so that Lord Arlbury can be taken back safely to Simbury Hall. After all, that is where he was staying before the two of you vanished, and that is where all the clothes and luggage he brought from London are still. I have sent a messenger to inform Lord and Lady Simbury that he will be arriving sometime today. Ellie, would you be so kind as to go with him?'

'Of course,' she replied, surprised that he should ask. It seemed obvious to her that she should continue in Philip's company, but then she remembered that Daniel knew very little of the bond that had formed between herself and Philip during the course of their adventures.

'What about Davey?' she remembered.

Daniel shook his head.

'My men say the lad has been weeping bitterly for his uncle all night. I will take him with me to Danbury and then I will see if I can find his mother.' He fidgeted, glancing towards the door. 'If you will excuse me, Ellie? There is so much for the gentry of the county to do to restore it to peace and heal the wounds of rebellion. At least the Duke of Monmouth, who caused all the trouble, has been captured and is being sent to London to face his uncle, King James.'

'I can cope,' Ellie assured him. 'Give my love to Mary and tell her I will see her soon.'

True to her word, she spent the next hour overseeing Philip's transfer to the large coach. The doctor had dosed him to give him a quiet night and he hardly stirred when he was carried from the bedroom to the well-padded interior of the coach — or during the hours that followed as they made their way towards Simbury. Once his eyes flickered and opened and she bent over him with a flask of water and murmured reassurance. His eyes barely seemed to focus on her face and he was soon asleep again.

★   ★   ★

It was almost nightfall when they reached their destination, just twenty-four hours after Philip had been facing the gallows as a rebel. Now when they reached the great house Lord and Lady Simbury were waiting to greet him and footmen carried him with the utmost tenderness to his room. Ellie stood to one side, apparently forgotten, till Philip had disappeared inside the house. Then Lady Simbury acknowledged her existence.

'Elgiva,' she said coldly, neglecting any words of greeting. 'You will want to go to your room. I will have food sent up to you.'

She turned away and made for the house, leaving Ellie to trail in her stately wake. In fact it suited Ellie to make for her familiar room where she could sink down in peace. After all, there was no one at Simbury House to whom she wished to speak. After a while, food was brought to her and later there was hot water before she went to bed. The maids simply curtseyed but did not speak to her and the same thing happened the following morning when she woke late, but Ellie took little notice of their behaviour because her mind was full of more important matters. She had to see Philip and find out how he was progressing, and then she wanted to send a messenger to Mary with a letter reassuring her that all was well and she had no reason to worry about her. And at some time, she remembered, she must try to find out more about the fortune which her aunt had left her. Well, first she would go to Philip's room.

It was only then, when she tried to open her bedroom door, that she discovered it was locked.

At first she shook it and twisted the handle, thinking that it might have stuck, but it did not yield. One of the maids must have somehow managed to lock it thoughtlessly, though she did not see how. Ellie thought she heard footsteps outside her room and called out to attract whoever was passing, but the steps halted and then retreated. Annoyed, she beat on the door with her fists, but it was some minutes before she heard a firm tread and the key turned in the lock. When it opened she found herself confronting Lady Simbury.

'You will oblige me,' said the lady

frostily, 'by stopping that clamour.'

'But I was locked in my room!' Ellie said furiously.

Lady Simbury raised her eyebrows.

'Of course you were. Did you expect to be given the liberty to roam the house, to mix with respectable women, to contaminate my daughters?'

Ellie stared at her.

'What are you talking about?'

Lady Simbury drew herself up to her full height.

'You have spent days — and nights — roaming the countryside together with an unmarried man, sleeping together with labourers and rebels. Your reputation is gone and you are a complete disgrace to your family. As soon as it can be arranged, you will be sent back to your father. He will have to deal with you.'

Ellie shook her head in bewilderment.

'But this is nonsense! Lord Arlbury and I were together because we were trying to escape from the rebels, that was all. Ask him!'

'Interrogate a sick man about a foolish girl who has ruined herself by pursuing him? I will do no such thing. You will stay in your room till you leave this house for ever.'

Swiftly she shut the door and Ellie heard the key turn in the lock. She leant against it, trying to grasp the mixture of deliberate misunderstanding and twisted logic that made up Lady Simbury's statement. One thing was clear, however. Her ladyship had found an excuse to rid herself of an encumbrance.

Ellie went to sit on her bed, huddled in misery. She had to admit that a malicious mind could make a very harmful story out of her adventures with Philip. Even if he defended her, there would be those who said it was a gentlemanly lie to protect her. But then she sat up and squared her shoulders. Lady Simbury could have intimidated the Ellie Colinridge of a week ago, but now she was dealing with a different girl; one who had faced armed soldiers and rebels and saved a man's life. She knelt by the door and checked the keyhole. As she had thought, Lady Simbury had taken the key with her. Well, locks could be picked, even if she had no idea how to do it. It took half an hour of experiments and attempts, with a scissor blade broken, before finally the tumblers clicked and she was free.

Presumably she was expected to be tearfully repenting her sins, for no guard had been left on her door. Swiftly she made her way to Philip's room, threw open the door and marched in. There was a squeal from a maid who dropped a pile of linen and a surprised gasp from the eldest Simbury daughter, Anne, who was clasping a handful of documents. Philip was in bed supported by pillows, the bed itself covered with more documents.

'You are supposed to be shut in your room!' exclaimed Anne Simbury. 'Dora, go and fetch my mother!'

The maid hurried out past Ellie, ignoring the fallen linen. Ellie smiled coolly at the other girl.

'If you do not follow her instantly, Anne Simbury, I shall throw you out.'

She advanced on the girl who stood her ground for a second only before gathering up her skirts and fleeing. Ellie swung round to Philip, who was regarding her with interest.

'What was that about?' he asked.

'Just a misunderstanding. You are recovering?'

He nodded.

'A few more good meals and I shall be up and about again. I don't know what argument you have with that girl, but thank you for getting rid of her. She titters.'

He stretched out a hand.

'Come here. I expected to see you by my bedside when I woke up, but I was told something had prevented you.'

'I came as soon as I was free,' she told him with careful truth.

'I'm afraid I can't remember everything that happened yesterday. Did we see Jem and Davey?'

'Yes. Davey is safe with Daniel.'

'And Jem?'

She shook her head and his lips tightened.

'He was a good man,' he said heavily.

'I see you are already busy,' she commented, gesturing at the documents.

'I thought I had better make a start on the mountain of correspondence.' He reached out and picked up one piece of paper. 'Incidentally, I have received a letter from King James telling me not to continue with any efforts I was making to win your hand in marriage, and that he will explain later.' He frowned. 'It is all very mysterious, and I hope he has explained to your father, but at least it means you are free, Ellie. Nobody is trying to marry us to each other against our will.'

She did not have time to analyse the mixture of emotions she felt, for at that moment the door opened wide and Lady Simbury appeared, followed by two footmen.

'Lord Arlbury,' she said, trying to smile at him and glare at Ellie at the same time, 'I am afraid Elgiva cannot stay with you any longer. She has other matters to see to. She will be leaving Simbury Hall soon to go to her father's.'

Philip looked startled, but then nodded understandingly.

'I suppose Sir Walter will want to see for himself that his daughter is safe.' He smiled at Ellie. 'Have a safe journey. Tell your father that I shall never forget my travelling companion.'

Ellie was tempted to tell him the real reason she was being dispatched to her father's house, but one look at Lady Simbury told her she would not be allowed to finish the first sentence of the story, and Philip, although cheerful, was still white-faced and weak. She bent to kiss him on the cheek before Lady Simbury's horrified eyes. 'Thank you. I shall go back to my room and pack now,' she told him, and saw Lady Simbury relax. In the doorway she turned for a last look at Philip. He was still smiling at her, but then Lady Simbury deliberately moved her bulk between them to block Ellie's view.

★ ★ ★

The lady of the house wasted no time. By late afternoon Ellie was in the family coach on her way to her father's house. No member of the Simbury family had said farewell; instead she had been escorted from her room by Lady Simbury's elderly maid who was now sitting in the coach with her and confining herself to monosyllabic replies when Ellie said anything to her. When they reached Sir Walter Colinridge's house Ellie went in search of her father while the maid went to find acquaintances in the servants' hall.

Sir Walter was, as she expected, in his library. He looked up in some surprise and she was sure that for a second he did not recognise her.

'Elgiva! This is unexpected. What are

you doing here?'

'Simbury House is busy with people planning action against the rebels, Father. Lady Simbury decided that I should come back here.'

'Oh? Is that so? Indeed. And pray tell me, how long will you be staying here?'

'I don't know yet.'

'Oh well, I expect you can fit in with our routine.' His eyes drifted back to his book and he did not look up when she left the library.

Her bags had been taken up to the room which she used on the few occasions she stayed at the house, but they had not been unpacked and the bed felt cold and damp. She summoned two maids and instructed one to unpack her bags and put her clothes away and the other to fetch a warming pan to air the bed. They performed their duties reluctantly and as they were leaving, she heard through the half-shut door one of them say, a little louder than was necessary, 'I doubt she needed a warming pan when she had Lord

Arlbury in her bed!'

As Ellie flushed crimson she heard the maids snigger and scurry away. Lady Simbury's maid had obviously wasted no time in spreading the story of her disgrace. She supped alone in her room.

* * *

The next morning she asked the housekeeper to have her room thoroughly cleaned and then a fire lit. The woman accepted her instructions but there was barely-veiled insolence in her manner. Ellie was growing angry. When she controlled her inheritance she would definitely set up her own establishment.

She did not see her father till they dined together. Occasionally he asked a polite question about what she knew of the rebellion, but the meal passed mostly in silence. Finally she steeled herself to broach a subject which might lead on to some awkward questions.

'Father, I must tell you that Lord Arlbury and I are not going to marry.'

He showed no surprise. 'Oh, I know that. One of His Majesty's secretaries sent me a scrawl explaining the mistake about the money.'

'What mistake?'

'Has no-one told you? The lawyer who informed the king that your Aunt Agatha died a rich woman was a little hasty. Her husband did leave her a fortune and that was when she drew up her will. Unfortunately since his death she has been investing the money in schemes doomed to failure. She died virtually penniless. I told you there was nothing to inherit.'

As Ellie's heart sank, he chuckled. 'I expect Arlbury could not wait to break off his courtship when he heard that.'

Ellie had lost her appetite. Philip had said the king had promised to explain later. Had he actually already received the explanation that there was no point in the earl marrying an insignificant girl with only a small inheritance to look forward to? Anyway, she would have to forget her dreams of her own establishment.

Matters did not improve during the days that followed. On one occasion when Ellie met the housekeeper she was struck by a brooch the woman was wearing. It was a gold brooch, unusually ornate even for an upper servant. The housekeeper saw Ellie looking at it and her hand went up, rather slowly, to cover the brooch.

'If I am not mistaken,' Ellie said carefully, 'that brooch looks like one that belonged to my mother.'

'It did,' said the woman, 'but Sir Walter gave it to me.'

Ellie's eyes widened and she stared at the housekeeper. It appeared that Sir Walter's activities had not all been limited to historical research. The housekeeper had doubtless made it clear that she was available when he wanted a little distraction. This would need considerable thought. But the housekeeper apparently did not wish to drop the subject.

'Sir Walter will confirm what I say. Ask him!'

If Ellie did, and her father had in fact given the brooch to the woman, it would change the housekeeper's status from paid servant to Sir Walter's acknowledged mistress. She had probably worn the brooch hoping to bring about just this confrontation. Ellie turned away silently, leaving the housekeeper still shrilly demanding that she speak to Sir Walter.

9

Could things get any worse? Ellie decided that on the whole she preferred the excitement and danger of the days she had shared with Philip Arlbury to the bleak prospect of the next twenty or thirty years spent in this house with a neglectful father and a woman who resented her very existence. She was also disappointed that she had heard nothing from Philip. No matter how busy he was, surely he could have sent her a brief message to confirm that he was still recovering, or even to thank her for saving his life? Surely she deserved that? Perhaps he blamed her for putting his life at risk in the first place.

A few more days passed. She rarely saw Sir Walter, the housekeeper was sulky and unco-operative, and the rest of the staff treated her as carelessly as they dared. Ellie decided that she would have to confront this problem soon and insist that she be treated with the respect due to her father's daughter. She hoped that her father would support her. After all, he had a high opinion of his own dignity. If that failed, she speculated desperately whether she could somehow find her way, via Bristol, to the colonies in America and start a completely new life.

Then one morning as she sat trying to convince herself that she enjoyed embroidering a cushion cover, she was told that there was a messenger waiting to see her. She leapt up, sure that Philip must have remembered her at last, but when she saw the man waiting for her she recognised him as one of Daniel Danbury's servants. He bowed before handing her a letter.

The missive was from Daniel, who wrote that he had only just learned of the way she had been treated by the Simburys and it expressed his anger at Lady Simbury's wilful misinterpretation of Ellie's days with Lord Arlbury.

He knew how little she had in common with her father, and invited Ellie to come to stay with Mary and himself as soon as possible — and for as long as she liked.

Ellie felt as if all her worries had been taken from her shoulders in one swoop.

'Is there a reply, mistress?' the messenger asked and she smiled at him.

'I will give the reply in person. I will come with you back to Danbury.'

Once again she ventured into the library.

'Father, the Danburys have invited me to stay with them, and I am leaving immediately.'

A gleam of hope appeared in her father's eyes.

'How long will you be staying there?'

'Indefinitely.'

'Ah!' He smiled. 'Well, I wish you a safe journey.'

Within an hour of the messenger's arrival, Ellie was riding pillion behind him on her way to Danbury.

Daniel greeted her with quiet warmth but Mary, heavily pregnant, threw her arms around her friend, happy tears rolling down her cheeks.

'Oh, Ellie, I've blamed myself every day for what happened to you!'

'Nonsense! I was running as fast as you. Anyway, it has all turned out well in the end.'

'Yes,' Mary said uncertainly, glancing sideways at her husband. Then she cheered up and patted her stomach. 'Only a few more weeks to go. I am so glad you will be here.'

Later, when Mary was resting, Daniel spoke to Ellie.

'The Earl of Arlbury returned to London soon after you left Simbury so he is not here to contradict Lady Simbury's stories, but I saw you with Arlbury and I know the truth. I have tried to combat Lady Simbury's wicked tongue, but I am afraid that too many people will always prefer scandal to sober truth.'

'You mean that for most people my reputation is in tatters and that I will no longer be acceptable in polite company,' Ellie said bluntly.

'It is possible, but while you are in my house I shall insist that you are treated with respect by everyone. You are very welcome here, Ellie, and from now on I shall regard you as one of my household.'

He was offering her shelter from shame.

Mary was also eager to discuss her problems.

'Daniel told me he was sure that nothing improper happened between you and Lord Arlbury,' she said. Was there a prurient gleam in her eye?

'Lord Arlbury and I shared a bed for three nights,' Ellie told her, and burst into laughter at her friend's shocked expression. 'Mary, it was the only way we could keep warm! For two of the nights I was more afraid that he would die than that he might try to make love to me!'

166

However when visitors called to see Mary, it was clear that Daniel had been right. They tended to treat Ellie coolly and even ignore her presence when they could. If Daniel was present, he would insist on drawing Ellie into the conversation, but Ellie did not want Mary to lose any friends on her account and so started to absent herself from the company when visitors came to the house.

It was a peaceful but rather boring existence. The rebels had been crushed and were now paying the price, with hundreds of them hanged or sentenced to transportation. Daniel reported that the Duke of Monmouth had been executed. Of course it was a fitting end for a traitor, but there was still a sense of shock that the king could put his own nephew to death.

Nothing had been heard from Philip Arlbury since he left Simbury. At Danbury everything now centred around Mary as she waited for the birth of her child, and she spent most of her time asleep.

Ellie was resigning herself to a future when she would be Aunt Ellie, a quiet figure in the background at Danbury who spent her time with the children and their mother. She would never have children of her own, of course, for there could be no suitors for a woman who would always have the shadow of a shameful past hanging over her.

At least, she comforted herself, she would not need financial charity. Her father would pay her an allowance, grateful that she was looked after elsewhere. Eventually she would inherit his estate, or what was left of it after the housekeeper had taken whatever she could, but she would probably still cling to the protection of Danbury and her only friends.

To divert herself, Ellie had started to pay attention to Danbury's rather neglected gardens, and her assistant in this new hobby was Davey. She had been surprised to see him still at Danbury but Daniel had explained that he had taken Davey home to his village, only to find Davey's mother in agonies of fear lest her son be arrested as a rebel. He had returned to Danbury with both mother and son and Davey was now living with his mother in a small cottage on the estate and working in the gardens. He still mourned his courageous Uncle Jem, but was generally happy with the way things had turned out for him.

10

One day a week or so later, Ellie had spent some hours weeding the herb garden where all her troubles had started and was taking a rest, sitting on a bench with her eyes closed so that she could better appreciate the aromas of the plants around her. Something made her open her eyes. Philip Arlbury was looking down at her.

Her first instinct was to spring up and greet him joyfully, and then she remembered that this was the Earl of Arlbury, the man who had apparently forgotten all about her as soon as she left Simbury. She rose slowly, smiled politely, and curtsied formally.

'My Lord Arlbury!'

He nodded curtly. Presumably he was embarrassed to find himself confronted with this minor figure from his past.

'I am afraid Master Danbury is out visiting a farm,' she informed him, 'and Mistress Danbury is asleep. She is soon to give birth, you will remember.'

He nodded again, and after waiting for him to speak Ellie's self-control gave way under the stress of her tumultuous emotions.

'Well, say something!' she snapped at him.

He looked at her with such fury in his eyes that she recoiled.

'I am speechless with anger,' he said, biting off each word. 'This morning I visited Simbury House to look for you, and I discovered that because of the few days we were forced to spend together fleeing for our lives, you are now disgraced and ostracised — rejected and sent back to your father.'

Ellie sank down on the bench.

'It was not your fault. It is the way that Lady Simbury thinks.'

Philip bared his teeth in a silent snarl.

'The lady may be more careful in future. I told Lord Simbury exactly what I thought of his wife's foul-minded gossip and the harm it had done you. I insisted that she make her mistake clear to everyone and redeem your reputation. I have the power to make Simbury's life uncomfortable in several ways, so I am confident that he will ensure that Lady Simbury does as I requested.'

Ellie blinked. 'That was kind of you.'

He seemed about to explode.

'Kind? She seemed to have overlooked the fact that she had portrayed me as a virtual rapist eager to take advantage of an inexperienced young girl.'

So he had been thinking of his own reputation, not of hers! Ellie bowed her head, but looked up sharply at his next words.

'I am almost as angry with you. Why didn't you inform me what the woman was doing? Danbury could have got a message to me! Instead you stupidly let the scandal spread unchecked.'

She looked up, indignantly blinking back tears.

'Why should I think you would care?

You were in London, busy with the king's affairs and had apparently forgotten all about me.'

'But I told you in my letter that I would come back to see you as soon as I was able to do so.'

'What letter?'

They looked at each other with dawning understanding.

'Now I understand why you greeted me so coldly! Did you really think I would not try to stay in contact with you? Before I left for London I gave a letter to Lady Simbury to send on to you. Of course I didn't know then what a poisonous and vindictive woman she is. She must have destroyed my message.'

Ellie was smiling now.

'At least, now I know that you didn't simply forget me as soon as I was out of your sight.'

She sighed, pushing back a wisp of hair, and stood up with a businesslike air. 'We will have a lot to talk about. Meanwhile, as the Danburys are unavailable, I must act as hostess. Let us go into the house and I will have refreshments served. I presume you are not staying at Simbury Hall. Where is the king sending you now?'

Philip did not move.

'The king did not send me. I have made it clear to His Majesty that I believe his treatment of the rebels has been totally wrong. He has been bent on revenge and as a result hundreds who were only guilty of folly have been slaughtered, as well as his brother's son. A little kindness, a little forgiveness, and he would have won the people's grateful loyalty. Instead, if there is another threat to the throne people will remember his ruthless cruelty.'

Then, for the first time, he smiled. 'Ask me why I have come here, Ellie.'

'Why have you come?' she said obediently.

'I have come to ask you to be my wife, to marry me.'

She looked at him in total disbelief.

'Are you joking? It is not in good taste.'

He shook his head.

'No, Ellie, I am very serious. Will you marry me?'

He paused, waiting for her answer.

'No,' she said flatly.

Clearly this was not the response he had expected.

'Why not?' he said indignantly.

'Because I am not going to marry you just to ease your conscience. You have discovered that my reputation is ruined because of you and you think marrying me will atone for that. Can you imagine what it would be like to be married to a man who would always resent being yoked to a woman he had not chosen willingly? And I do not want a husband who would expect eternal gratitude from me because he had saved me from shame!'

Philip sighed. 'And I thought you were an intelligent woman! I am certainly not prepared to sacrifice myself just because of the ill-natured gossip of a stupid woman like Lady Simbury! You once told me that the lady I chose would be very fortunate if she married me of her own free will. I want you to do that, not because you feel that you have to.'

'Then why do you want to marry me?'

He shrugged. 'For several reasons. You are an intelligent young woman, presentable and well-bred. You are healthy, so should produce healthy children. You have been reared modestly without extravagant habits, and your upbringing should suit you for a quiet life in the country rather than the court.'

'How practical — and cold-blooded. You sound as if you are choosing a horse, not a wife! Anyway, there are hundreds of better-born and richer young women who would meet your requirements. I suppose you know my great inheritance was a myth?'

'Oh yes — your unfortunate Aunt Agatha. Ellie, I am very rich. I do not need a wealthy wife, but I do want a healthy, intelligent one.'

She looked at him suspiciously. This could not be all.

'Philip Arlbury, if you do not tell me at once why you really want to marry me, I shall attack you physically!'

'Just like you attacked that poor soldier with a horseshoe?' He looked at her soberly. 'I knew this would be hard. If we had had longer to get to know each other, you would know my reasons without having to ask. Ellie, the truth is that I want to marry you very much, but I am not very good at expressing my emotions and this is the first time I have asked anyone to marry me. I am in fact finding it very difficult.'

She took his hand. 'Please tell me, as well as you can,' she coaxed.

'I believe we suit each other, that we would support each other through the years. We would be honest with each other. We would be man and wife, Philip and Ellie, because to you I am just a man named Philip, not the Earl of Arlbury. We would be partners — equals.'

'Is there any other reason?'

He took a deep breath.

'One more reason, and it is important. Do you remember those three nights we spent together when you held me to keep me warm? Every night I dream that you are beside me, and I turn to take you in my arms, and it breaks my heart when you are not there.'

They looked at each other.

'I will marry you, Philip Arlbury,' Ellie said softly.

He exhaled deeply, and then looked at her challengingly in his turn.

'Why?'

She looked at him with a half-smile.

'Well, in spite of your arrogance you are very rich, an earl, and the lord of vast estates. If I marry you I will be a great lady with all the jewels and gowns I could wish for. Marriage to you would definitely be preferable to spending the rest of my life at Danbury as Aunt Ellie.'

'Have you any other reason?'

A blush rose in her cheeks.

'I want to share your bed for the rest of my life.'

He threw back his head and closed his eyes as if he could scarcely contain his joy. 'I will make you happy, Ellie, I promise you.'

'I know you will. You do realise, of course, that sometimes we will quarrel furiously?'

'And then we will make up.'

'Being married to you will not be dull. Oh . . . !' She hesitated suddenly.

'What is the matter?'

'Before we can start being happy together, we will have to get married, and that means that I shall have to tell my father that after being apparently betrothed to you, and then not being betrothed, I am once again going to marry you.'

Philip waved airily.

'There is no need. I told him that when I called on him, looking for you. After all, you should be married from your father's house.'

Ellie gaped inelegantly.

'You told him? What was his reaction?'

Philip frowned. 'I forget. I was trying to discover where you had gone.'

'Did you by any chance meet his housekeeper? I am not sure she will co-operate gladly in arranging our wedding.'

Philip brushed this aside also.

'She will be no match for my mother, who will probably be arriving within the week. She is looking forward very much to meeting my bride and helping to arrange our wedding.'

Ellie looked at him with dangerous calm. 'You arranged all this before you had even proposed to me? Was I the last person to know that I was going to marry you? Weren't you being just a little over-confident, my lord?'

He grinned.

'Not over-confident, just determined. I had resolved that I would not leave here until you had agreed to marry me, even if it meant Danbury begging you to accept me just so he could get rid of me. I was prepared to be romantic, tragic, pleading. I was going to shower you with rich gifts.'

Ellie raised an eyebrow.

'Rich gifts? Perhaps I accepted you too quickly.'

'You can have them as presents to my bride. And now . . . ' He took her hands in his and drew her towards him — only to turn impatiently when he was interrupted by a cry from an agitated maidservant who was running down the path towards them.

'Mistress Colinridge, come quickly! It's the mistress, she's having her baby!'

Ellie gasped. 'Mary is in labour? I must go to her!'

But Philip kept tight hold of her hands.

'Not so quick, my lady. Even I know that these things usually take hours. Mary Danbury can very well spare you the time for our first kiss.'

Smiling, Ellie closed her eyes and lifted her face up to his, and Philip took her into his arms.

We do hope that you have enjoyed reading this large print book.

Did you know that all of our titles are available for purchase?

We publish a wide range of high quality large print books including:
Romances, Mysteries, Classics
General Fiction
Non Fiction and Westerns

Special interest titles available in large print are:
The Little Oxford Dictionary
Music Book, Song Book
Hymn Book, Service Book

Also available from us courtesy of Oxford University Press:
Young Readers' Dictionary
(large print edition)
Young Readers' Thesaurus
(large print edition)

For further information or a free brochure, please contact us at:
Ulverscroft Large Print Books Ltd.,
The Green, Bradgate Road, Anstey,
Leicester, LE7 7FU, England.
Tel: (00 44) 0116 236 4325
Fax: (00 44) 0116 234 0205

When Melanie Crighton started her new job as companion to Chloe, Jake Masters' young daughter, it wasn't long before employer and worker became strongly attracted to each other. But this love affair could have no happy ending. Jake's magnetic personality ensured that he had an endless supply of admirers in his life, and Melanie feared that she was to be only one of his many 'affairs'. There was also the problem of his elusive wife Marion to consider . . .

THE ENDURING FLAME

Denise Robins

Inside his log cabin, in the Great White Wilderness, young Joanna Grey's father dies, and she's forced to flee from the lecherous Conrad Owen into the icy wilderness. Lost and exhausted, she's found by Richard Strange and they shelter in a cabin where they become trapped by raging snowstorms. And, despite discovering their love for one another, they agree that John should return to his wife. But then, terrifyingly for Joanna alone in the arctic night, Conrad Owen appears . . .

CHALLENGING LOVE

Eileen Barry

Keith Chilton was a shy young man. Dedicated to tracing a disease that had killed off a beloved relative, he valued the peace and security of his laboratory and the use of the library in his uncle's house. Then his uncle died and bequeathed the house and library to Keith provided he got himself married. Overcoming his reluctance, he began to meet likely young women . . . only to fall in love with the mysterious Rachel Beamish, his grey-haired, severe, bespectacled secretary . . .

A POINT OF PRIDE

Liz Fielding

Six years before, Casey had adored one of her father's workmen, Gil Blake. But realising she would just be another notch on his bedhead she'd threatened to get him sacked. Now, with her father about to go bankrupt, he's back and she still loves him. But Gil, clearly no longer a builder's labourer, is still angry and wants revenge: Gil whistles and Casey is obliged to dance to his tune. And the moment she stops, her parents will suffer . . .